Copyright © 2024 by Theophilus Monroe.

All rights reserved. Printed in the United States of America. No part of this book may be used or reproduced in any manner whatsoever without written permission except in the case of brief quotations embodied in critical articles or reviews.

Cover Design by Deranged Doctor Design

Proofreading/Editing by Mel: https://getproofreader.co.uk/

This book is a work of fiction. Names, characters, businesses, organizations, places, events and incidents either are the product of the author's imagination or are used fictitiously. Any resemblance to actual persons, living or dead, events, or locales is entirely coincidental.

For information:

www.theophilusmonroe.com

THE FURY OF A VAMPIRE WITCH
BOOK 7

BLOODY HEARTS

THEOPHILUS MONROE

Chapter 1

The night air was heavy with the threat of rain as we barreled down the slick streets of downtown Providence, our SUVs a dark convoy snaking towards Ridley Hotel. Reports indicated strange orgies and bloodshed. Instant passion turned murderous. Mug Ruith (aka Muggs)—my druid-vampire progeny—believed it was the work of a cupid. No, not a little angel. A hideous chaos monster.

Muggs, in the back seat, had inexplicably decided this was the ideal moment to trim his toenails.

Click. Click. Click.

Gag! Gag! Gag!

"Seriously, Muggs?" I grumbled. "Now?"

"When my feet hit the ground, I need to be ready."

Muggs was the only blind vampire I'd ever heard of. Usually when someone becomes a vampire, their bodies heal. Any previous disabilities go away. That was the case with Mel, who'd had fibromyalgia before I sired her. When I turned Muggs, though, even if becoming a vampire healed him physically, his vision never returned.

My best explanation? He was so old *before* he was turned that his brain just didn't know how to handle visual stimuli. Or maybe his optical nerve was already so deteriorated that there was nothing left to heal. Whatever the case, his blindness came with a few perks. Becoming a vampire usually heightens one's senses. Since he was blind, his other senses advanced to superhero levels.

Muggs could hear an insect's wings buzz from a half-mile away. He could feel the air shift or the ground vibrate when someone or something moved. And if someone farted in a crowd... Let's just say that not everything to do with his sensory adaptation was pleasant.

"You need to be ready?" Mel chimed in, her lips quirking in the rearview mirror. "We're going to battle with a cupid. You're not doing a foot-shoot for your OnlyFans."

"Hey! Some people are into gnarly feet! I'm making good money from that page!"

I rolled my eyes. "You can't be serious. And how the hell are you operating a website, anyway? *You can't see* and don't know shit about using a computer!"

Mel cleared her throat. "I plead the fifth."

I glared at Mel. "I didn't even ask you if you'd helped him. But that answers my question."

"Don't blame Mel," Muggs added. "It's just a little side hustle. I like having my own money. We thought I could make a little extra dough this way."

"With your nasty hooves?" I almost gagged imagining what his page might look like. "Why would you think anyone wants to see that?"

"Because people are weird!" Mel piped up. "And weird, lonely people will pay anything to entertain their secret... feet-ishes."

I didn't know how to respond to that. "First, if you needed money, you could have just asked. Second, if you wanted your own money, which I get, you could have just joined a goddamn MLM. Sell body lotions, magic weight loss pills, or kitchenware like most people do."

Muggs shuddered. "No way! Those markets are saturated. Everyone knows you can't make money with an MLM unless you get in *early*."

I cocked an eyebrow. "And you think you can compete with cute girls and their pretty little tootsies by selling pictures of your old man feet?"

"It's a niche market!" Muggs sighed. "Trust me, I know what I'm doing."

Mel was giggling uncontrollably as she navigated the streets. This was *her* doing. I glared at her. "I can't believe you put him up to this."

"Don't worry about it, Mercy," Muggs piped up. "I won't leave my clippings on the ground. They're already paid for. I have to save them and send them out to my fans!"

It was a good thing I hadn't recently fed—because I had a sudden urge to vomit out the passenger side window. "Just put your damn socks and shoes back on."

"Mercy!" Muggs protested. "I need to make sure all my senses are perfectly calibrated before a fight. If my feet aren't in perfect condition, I might misinterpret the vibrations coming from the ground."

I raised an eyebrow as I craned my neck back toward Muggs. "Don't cupids fly?"

Muggs nodded resolutely. "They do. But when you're facing a cupid, you also have to deal with the chaos that surrounds them. We'll need to be on high alert."

Cupid. The very name conjured images of chubby-cheeked cherubs from Valentine's Day cards, but the reality was far more hideous. Muggs couldn't tell us exactly what they looked like, but he knew they were nasty. I didn't question it. Given Muggs' recent entrepreneurial efforts, *nasty* was his specialty.

"Mercy, remember—" Muggs began, his voice grave as he finally laced his boots and locked eyes with me in the rearview mirror. "Cupids aren't angelic matchmakers. They *use* what *feels* like love to inspire chaos. When everyone becomes obsessed with each other, jealousy soon follows. The obsession is so strong that it inevitably turns homicidal."

"Then we need to end this quick." My hand instinctively reached for my wand strapped to my thigh.

"Antoine, Alice, and the rest are ready," Mel informed us, her voice a steady beacon in the dark. "Plus, we have Juliet and her younglings. We've got the numbers, Mercy. We can do this."

"Numbers won't mean squat if we can't contain it," I countered, my thoughts racing. "There's really only one way to kill these things, right?"

Muggs nodded. "Shoot the bastard through the heart with its own arrow. Nothing else will do."

I nodded. "Then we focus on containment. If we can't kill the bastard without a cupid's arrow of our own, we trap it."

"How are we going to do that?" Mel asked, steering the SUV into a right turn.

"My *enerva* spell might neutralize the creature," I mused aloud. "And Muggs, you'll need to be ready with a portal. If I can stop the cupid, you can whisk it away to a cell back at the Underground."

"Sounds like a plan." Muggs popped his knuckles. "I'll have the portal ready. But with my spirit-gaze, I'll only be able to see the cupid's arrows once they're fired. Something about their quivers shrouds their magic from my druidic sight. I'll be relying on my other senses to locate the cupid. If you immobilize the creature, I won't be able to zero in on the flutter of its wings."

"Then, when I hit the bastard with my spell, you'll be able to sense the residue of my magic in the cupid. Use my magic to focus your portal."

Muggs nodded. "Good thinking. That should work. Just give me the signal."

As Mel pulled our SUV around the corner, the Ridley Hotel loomed into view. And what a shitshow it was. The neon sign flickered erratically, mirroring the chaos beneath it. Likely strangers turned to couples courtesy of the cupid's arrows were tangled together against the brick façade, kissing with a fervor that would make a succubus blush. Nearby, a brawl had erupted, fists flying with a lover's passion turned violent.

It was like V-Day met D-Day.

A fist connecting to a jaw sent blood splattering on the sidewalk. I could smell it from inside the SUV. My stomach growled in response.

"Juliet, you see this?" I clicked my earpiece to life, connecting with Juliet via comms. She and a few of the younglings she'd brought with her to the team were just behind us in another SUV. "Your younglings doing alright?"

"Everyone fed before we left," my vampire girlfriend responded through the comms, her tone sharp as broken glass. "I think we'll be fine, but we should get in and out of here as fast as possible."

"Removing the cupid from the scene won't end the violence," Muggs added, also through comms. "Kill the cupid with an arrow from the same quiver that infected the victims, and it should break the spell over the people. But we can't do that until we capture the little devil."

"Antoine, you copy?" I spoke into the comms, checking for our rear guard. Alice was riding with him, probably feeling sorry for herself. Ever since Ladinas left us—taking the djinn's place in its lamp for a century in order to save *my* life—she barely spoke to me. But we needed her help. And what better way to get over heartbreak than to eviscerate a cupid with her katanas? No, her blades couldn't kill a cupid, but dismemberment had to be worth something.

"Copy, Mercy," came the deep, calm response. "Just let us know how to proceed."

"The plan is simple. We move in carefully. We need to stay on the lookout for the cupid. Try to avoid the victims. Best stay out of the fray if possible. But if we have to deal with human interference, non-lethal force only."

"Understood," Antoine added.

"Jinx?" I evoked Juliet's nickname to confirm she was on board with the plan.

"Non-lethal? No fun, Mercy."

"I trust you're joking," I grunted. Truth is, I wasn't sure she was. I didn't know her that well, all things considered. The feelings we had for each other were probably just as artificial as those manufactured by a cupid's arrow. Juliet and I shared a blood bond. An attraction that results when two vampires feed on the same victim, then on each other.

I'd never had a girlfriend before. I'd only ever dated men. The blood bond elicited feelings between Juliet and me I'd never experienced. It didn't really matter, though. I mean, maybe our relationship was based on a chemical reaction. But don't most relationships start that way? What's really the difference between hormones and a blood bond? And who was I to say our feelings weren't real? What's the difference? If you feel something, it's real by definition.

And I was *happy* with Juliet. Happier than I'd been with anyone since... well... ever!

But as the ex-girlfriend of my dead vampire-brother Jector, aka Jack the Ripper, there was a lot about Juliet's past I didn't know. As a vampire, regardless of her past, the idea that she might enjoy the occasional homicide wasn't entirely out of character. And that she used to date a serial *eviscerator...*

I did my best to push the thought out of my mind. I used to date Ramon, after all. His penchant for dismemberment didn't make *me* like him. Even if I was guilty of entertaining his proclivities once or twice through the years. It would be hypocritical to judge Juliet by the people she used to love. Who doesn't have a crazy ex? Dating a sociopath is a goddamn rite of passage. Especially for vampires.

"Whatever," I piped up. "We have to stay on task. That means we don't harm any humans. The goal is to capture and neutralize the cupid."

"We'll have to find the thing first," Antoine's voice echoed back at me through my earpiece.

"Let's park a few blocks away," I suggested. "We'll move in on foot, nice and quiet. Get a lay of the land first."

"Copy that," Mel grunted from the driver's seat, her hands firm on the wheel as she swung our SUV into an inconspicuous alleyway. The dim glow of streetlights cast long shadows over the dashboard.

"Keep your senses sharp," I spoke into the comms, my eyes scanning the old brick façades that lined the streets. "Especially you, Muggs. We need those ears of yours."

"Already on it," Muggs replied. "Ears are open. Toes are trimmed. I'm ready."

"Remember, no one goes in alone. Cupid's arrows can mess with your head," I warned them, stepping out onto the pavement, the cold air sending a chill through my undead flesh. My boots clicked against the concrete as we moved toward Ridley Hotel, each step deliberate, each breath measured—even though I didn't technically need to breathe. Some human habits die hard—even if it was over 130 years since I *technically* died.

"Juliet, how are the younglings holding up?" I asked, keeping my tone even, not wanting to betray any concern.

"Restless but ready," Juliet responded, her voice carrying the confidence of a seasoned warrior despite her youthful vampires' inexperience.

"Good. Keep 'em tight." I could feel my fangs throb in response to the savory scent of blood that wafted past my nostrils in the breeze. If it was affecting me, it was going to be twice as difficult for the younglings. "Doing alright, Mel?"

"Peachy, love," Mel snickered. "It's like we just arrived at the Golden Corral. All you can eat. Arteries on tap."

"We aren't here to feast," I reminded her. "I know it smells... delicious."

"We all need to focus," Muggs piped in. "We can't let the blood in the air distract us from our purpose."

I nodded back at Muggs, who was only a few paces to my right. Of course, he couldn't see my nod, but whatever. It wasn't the first time I forgot that my non-verbals were lost on the blind vampire-druid.

"Antoine, status?"

"Bringing up the rear. All clear so far."

"Keep it that way. We can't afford a blind spot." I could hear the gravel under his tires as he rolled slowly in our wake, a steady thrum of vigilance.

We moved forward, the streetlamps casting an eerie glow on the chaos unfolding around Ridley Hotel. Couples entwined with such passion they seemed oblivious to the world collapsing into bedlam around them. A few feet away, a brawl erupted—two men, shirts torn and faces bloodied, locked in a dance of violence over a woman who watched with glazed eyes.

"Stay sharp, team," I ordered through the comms. "Remember, these people are not themselves."

"Encountering increased hostility up ahead," Juliet's voice crackled through the earpiece. "Some of these guys are throwing punches like they've got personal vendettas."

"Non-lethal force only," I reminded her. "They're victims here."

"Understood."

A scream pierced the night, and I turned toward the sound. A man whose eyes burned with an unnatural fervor pinned a woman against a wall. The cupid hit the man, it seemed, but the arrow hadn't struck the woman to manipulate her consent.

My stomach twisted in disgust. I hadn't thought about *that* effect of a cupid's chaos-inducing attacks.

With a flick of my wrist and a whispered *enerva,* energy sizzled from my wand, enveloping the aggressor. He slumped to the ground, the madness temporarily quenched.

"Nice shot," Muggs said, helping the woman to her feet.

"Let's keep moving," I urged, scanning the shadows for the source of this mayhem. "We need to find that Cupid before more people get hurt."

We continued moving through the chaos. People were doing it in the road, against buildings, even in the gutters. Some trysts interrupted by jealous cupid-infected onlookers. Half of them were stark naked in the streets.

There's nothing quite like seeing two men fight with hard-ons. Like the worst fencing match ever. On guard!

I'd have laughed about it more if the result wasn't so deadly. That cupid had to be nearby. But where was the wily little fucker?

Finally, a flicker of movement caught my eye, a flutter that didn't belong to the wind. "There," I hissed, pointing to the grotesque winged figure perched atop the hotel marquee. Muggs was right. It wasn't a cute little cherub. The cupid was the second ugliest thing I'd seen all day. Next to Mugg's calloused foot. The misshapen creature had bulbous red eyes and twisted features; its wings were ragged and matted and its skin a sickly shade of gray. It held what looked like an impossibly delicate bow in one hand and drew an arrow from a dark quiver hanging from its back. The cupid nocked his arrow and immediately pink flames burst from the tip and spread down the shaft.

"Team Two, flank left. We need it away from the humans," I commanded, my voice steady. "Try to distract him, but keep cover and don't get shot."

"Got it, Mercy," Juliet's voice crackled through the comms, her tone all business now. "Moving into position."

Muggs grunted from behind, and I turned just in time to see an arrow—sleek, twisted, and barbed—pierce his ancient flesh. It struck him square in the ass, and before the groan escaped his lips, another arrow found its mark on Mel's back. My mouth dropped open in horror as they turned to each other, their movements suddenly languid and deliberate. It felt like it happened in slow motion. But before I could do a damn thing, Muggs pressed his crinkled lips to Mel's.

I threw up a little in my mouth.

"Shit!" I cursed into comms, the sight jarring me to my core. "Where did that come from? Another cupid must be around here. Muggs and Mel were shot!"

"Mercy!" Juliet's urgent shout sliced through my disgust like an icy blade. "We're screwed! Look up!"

My gaze snapped to where she pointed, and there they were—three more Cupids circling above us, their arrows nocked and ready to unleash hell upon us.

"Damn it," I spat, realizing our mistake. "Forget cornering one of them—they have *us* surrounded! Everyone take cover!"

I ducked behind a nearby car, my grip tightening on my wand. The three Cupids, their faces now twisted into cruel smiles, darted through the air with unnatural grace. Muggs and Mel were still locked in their embrace. I didn't want to look. It was... disturbing. But it was one of those things that's so damn weird you can't help but stare.

"Mercy, we're running out of time," Juliet's voice crackled over the comms. "I've got the first cupid we were tracking in my sights, but I can't take him down without you or Muggs."

"Ten four," I replied. "I'll try to get to you. We can't take down all these bastards, but maybe if we can capture one of them, we can use its arrows to kill the rest."

I could run fast. No matter how skilled a cupid's aim, hitting a moving target had to be harder than one that's standing still. Without giving it a second thought, I sprung up from behind the car and darted toward Juliet.

But then a reflection of light caught my eye—the streetlight reflecting from Alice's twin blades as she charged past Muggs and Mel (still locked in an embrace) toward the cupid that shot them.

"Alice!" I screamed. "Take cover!"

She didn't respond. I knew she could hear me. Even if she wasn't listening on comms—which she should have been—with vampiric hearing, there's no way she didn't hear my order. But she *chose* to ignore me. The foolish, insolent bitch.

I stopped in my tracks. "Damn it. I have to help Alice. She's going to get herself shot!"

"Mercy!" Juliet screamed back through comms. "She can handle herself. If we don't catch this one--"

But before I could decide, a pink arrow shot through the air and caught Alice right in her thigh.

Alice winced and grabbed at the wound. Then she looked up and fixed her eyes on Muggs.

Shit...

"The druid is mine!" Alice screamed as she grabbed Mel from behind.

Mel went flying. Alice was a lot older than she was. "No, bitch! The doggone druid is mine!"

Mel crashed against a parked car, setting of its alarm. But that didn't dissuade her warped desire. "No, he's mine, mine, mine!"

It reminded me of that awful Michael Jackson / Paul McCartney duet from the *Thriller* album. And to make it worse, they were fighting over *Muggs!*

"Screw this," I shouted through comms. "Abandon the mission. If we don't separate Mel and Alice, they'll kill each other."

"If we don't catch one of them and get their arrows, we won't be able to break the spell!" Juliet protested. "You want to save Mel, Muggs, and Alice? Help me catch this motherfucker!"

I clenched my fists. "Antoine. Grab Mel and get out of here."

"Mel? What about Muggs and Alice?"

"I can deal with Mel and Muggs. Hopefully, my sire bond can overpower their... urges. But Alice is too strong to capture, and she'll kill Mel if we don't separate them."

Antoine gave the order to his team and they sprung into action. Saving Mel was the top priority. We'd worry about dealing with Muggs and Alice later. Juliet was right, though. Even if we managed to separate them, without a cupid's arrow, we couldn't kill the bastard that shot them. If we couldn't do that, their obsession would only worsen.

If I was going to help Juliet catch this cupid, I'd have to do it without Muggs. Could *enerva* keep a cupid down long enough to capture it, or at least steal its quiver? We didn't have a choice. This *had* to work.

I ran as fast as I could and met Juliet and her younglings behind a parked FedEx truck.

Everyone was armed, but these younglings weren't trained yet. Bullets wouldn't kill the cupid, but if we could hit it, we could slow it down. Enough that I could blast it with my spell and take its arrows.

"Can you give me cover?" I asked, kneeling beside Juliet.

She nodded. "We can try. But Mercy, we don't know if these bullets will do a damn thing against a cupid."

I kissed Juliet on the cheek. "It's a risk we have to take. Watch my six. The last thing we need is for another cupid to catch me from behind."

We didn't have time to argue strategy. With Mel, Muggs, and Alice already infected and locked in a deadly lust triangle, every minute lost made it less likely we'd get out of this predicament with our team intact.

My wand extended toward the little bastard, still perched over the words "Ridley Hotel" in neon. Juliet and her younglings fired at the cupid, littering the brick wall behind him with bullet holes.

"*Enerva!* I screamed. But as the magic blasted out of the tip of my wand, a blazing pink streak flew back at me. My spell hit its mark, the wounded cupid falling from his perch onto the sidewalk. But as fast as I was, my attempt to twist away from the arrow backfired.

He shot me in the ass. Left cheek.

"Fuck!" It hurt like a son of a bitch. I dropped to one knee.

"Mercy!" Juliet's cry sounded like it came from a hundred yards away. But I could feel her hand on my shoulder.

I twisted my head to look at her. Our eyes met.

But I felt nothing. We were already bound in blood. At least we had been. I assumed the cupid's arrow would double the effect. Instead, it was like I was looking at a stranger. Even though I knew exactly who she was. Even though I remembered how I felt about her just seconds before.

"Juliet?"

"Are you alright? What are you feeling?"

I shook my head. "I don't know. The arrow isn't affecting me like it is everyone else. I don't know…"

The arrow that hit me was already gone. They dissipated on contact. We still needed to get the cupid's quiver.

Juliet released a deep breath. "We're sitting ducks out here. There are at least three more cupids out there, and we don't know how long your spell will keep that little guy down."

I rose to my feet, massaging my sore glute. "You're right. Let's grab the cupid and get the hell out of here. We still need to save Mel and Muggs."

"And Alice," Juliet reminded me.

My head fell. "Right. Alice."

Juliet kissed my forehead. I still felt *nothing*. Had the cupid's arrow somehow canceled out the effect of our blood bond? I didn't have much of a working heart at all—and I certainly didn't have the heart to tell Juliet what I was feeling. All I knew was that we had to stick to the plan. We'd worry about the effects of the cupid's arrow on *me* later.

Chapter 2

We failed. Three cupids (at least) were still out there, firing their arrows at will. Muggs and Alice were gone, lost in their lust. At least Antoine and the team rescued Mel before Alice could behead my favorite progeny.

And Juliet and I *did* manage to capture a cupid and its quiver. We didn't meet our objective to neutralize the cupid threat, but all wasn't lost. With the cupid's arrows in our possession, we had a chance.

My chest was cold. I felt nothing for Juliet. It was like the cupid's arrow had sapped my capacity for love. Antoine and the team were dealing with Mel and the unconscious cupid. As I walked like a ghost down the halls of the Underground, my mind and heart numb, Juliet sneaked up behind me and grabbed my hand. I pulled mine away. Not on purpose. It was almost by instinct.

"Mercy? What's wrong?"

I sighed. "I'm sorry. Just not in the mood for affection."

It wasn't exactly a lie. But it was a partial truth.

"You're worried about Mel and Muggs."

I nodded. "Even Alice. It's one thing for a crowd of humans to turn violent, but Alice... she's deadly."

"And with Muggs' magic, there's no telling how much damage he could do if his passions turn violent."

"You're right," I nodded curtly as I rubbed my butt again. "Damn, it still hurts."

"You seriously aren't feeling anything after being hit by the cupid's arrow?"

"I feel nothing." Juliet didn't realize how accurate that statement was. It was like one moment my heart was swollen with love, about to burst, and the next moment it was an empty tomb.

"I don't understand. How are you immune to the cupid's magic?"

I snorted. "I don't know if I'm immune to it. Maybe it just affected me differently."

"But why?" Juliet pursed her lips. "Because you're a witch?"

I shrugged. "It's not unheard of. Sometimes witches are affected by magic differently. I'd cast a spell just milliseconds before the arrow hit me. Sometimes when magics combine in a witch, the results can be unpredictable."

Juliet put her arm around me and pulled me close. It took all my willpower not to push her away. "Maybe your magic protected you. You may have dodged a bullet."

I chuckled a little. "Well, I didn't dodge that arrow."

Juliet leaned in and kissed me on the cheek. I forced a smile. "I'd love to sit here and chat about it, but I need to try to help Mel. I'm hoping my sire bond can counter the effects of the cupid's magic. Then, we need to figure out how we can use the cupid and its arrows to take down the rest."

"You're right." Juliet stood and straightened her shirt. "How can I help?"

I rested a hand on Juliet's shoulder. I was hoping another touch might bring back what I felt for her before. It didn't work. "Make sure the younglings are well fed. Make sure everyone's ready to go. If I can figure out how to use the cupid's arrows we'll need to mobilize straight away."

"Got it!" Juliet said and started to leave. "And Mercy?"

I swallowed hard. "Yeah?"

"Happy Valentine's Day!"

I cocked my head. What a goddamn coincidence. Cupids on Valentine's Day. Or maybe it wasn't one at all. The wheel of the year turns, the convergence between worlds opens the earth up to new threats. Maybe cupids were associated with V-day for a reason. "Yeah, Jinx. You, too."

I released a drawn-out sigh as Juliet disappeared around the corner. Real love evaded me for more than a century.

But you know what they say. Better to have loved and lost than...

Fuck that. It's total bullshit.

Heartbreak is *supposed* to hurt. It hurts because your heart still desires what it had. But this was worse than that. It was cold. Empty. I was like a dead woman walking—deader than I'd ever been, even as a vampire.

I wasn't even *worried* about Mel and Muggs. I certainly didn't give two shits about Alice. I didn't care about anything. But my mind and memories were still there. I knew I was *supposed* to care. I vaguely recalled *how* it felt to love.

I knew that if I didn't handle my shit and do what I needed to do, I'd *hate* myself later. If my feelings ever returned.

Fake it until you make it, Mercy.

That was the motto *de jour*.

What else could I do? Sit on my ass and do nothing at all? The idea was more tempting than it should have been.

But that was the least of my worries. The last time I felt anything like this, when Oblivion took me over, I nearly destroyed everyone and everything I ever cared about. Not to mention the world. The only difference now was that I didn't have an evil dragon bent on flushing all existence into the void, whispering sweet nothings in my ear.

But I knew enough to realize how dangerous I could be when I didn't give a shit.

All I could think to do was let Juliet's voice be my guide. If I didn't have a conscience, no inner-voice in my swollen dome telling me what's right or wrong, I'd usually consult with Ladinas or Muggs. Maybe even Mel. But now that Ladinas was stuck in a djinn's lamp and Muggs and Mel were both under the influence, all I could do was hope Juliet wouldn't lead me astray. That it was the Juliet I used to love who'd be my compass—not Jack the Ripper's former ex and partner in mutilation.

First things first. I had to try to get Mel's head right. I didn't have a clue if it would work. I'd seen a vampire's sire bond do some pretty incredible things, but the truth was, I never enjoyed using my sire bond on my progenies. In my experience, using any kind of mind-control or manipulation had a tendency to backfire. Just because I could command my progeny to do something didn't mean they wouldn't resent me for it.

To force anyone to do something they don't want to do doesn't accomplish much beyond *temporary compliance*. You can't force an addict to get sober unless they want it for themselves. You can't make anyone do anything they don't want to do without expecting a little backlash.

When it came to younglings, well, sometimes it was necessary to take advantage of the bond. A parent can't just let a child do whatever they want. Sometimes exerting one's authority is necessary for the child's benefit. Even then, though, backlash is inevitable. It usually comes in the form of a fit or a breakdown. The same was true of vampire babies. But sometimes it was a measured decision. I knew I'd get a tantrum, but what of it? Try to parent a child by giving them whatever they want just to avoid tantrums and you'll raise a spoiled brat.

There was a chance it wouldn't work. That the cupid's influence would be too strong to counter. But I had to try.

Because the cupid's influence was more manipulative than anything I could force Mel to do by sire bond. I also knew her well enough to know she didn't *want* to play tonsil hockey with Muggs.

She might have a tantrum. The cupid's influence might stoke her anger when I tried it. But she'd thank me later.

Mother knows best.

Antoine had Mel locked up in one of our cells. The walls were three feet thick, steel bars surrounded by concrete. The doors were virtually impenetrable and any attempt to manipulate the door sent a blast of artificial sunlight into the room. One of Demeter's old designs that Mel installed herself. Hopefully she didn't know a workaround. Mel didn't have the brute strength to break out of the cell, but she was a clever little girl.

Thankfully I found her reclined against the wall, pantomiming plucking petals from an invisible rose.

"Muggs loves me... he loves me not... he loves me... loves me not. He *loves me!!!!*"

I rolled my eyes. "But you don't love him."

"I do, Mercy! I really do! He's the one!" Mel sprang to her feet and ran to me with wide eyes.

That's all it took. My gaze locked onto hers. "You don't love Muggs, Mel."

Mel tilted her head. "I don't?"

"You don't."

"Well…" Mel pursed her lips as if in deep thought. Then her eyes shot wide. "Christ. You're right!"

I exhaled in relief. "Glad to have you back. Wasn't sure that would work."

"Oh it did, Mercy! You don't know how well it worked! I see everything clearly now!"

"You do?" I bit my lip. There was still something off. Something in the cadence of her voice, the way she looked at me.

Mel took my hands. Then she hugged me.

Ugh. I've never been much of a hugger, but best to go along with it given Mel's tenuous condition. I patted her back three times.

Then she grabbed my ass.

"I love *you,* Mercy!!!!"

Before I realized it, she'd pressed her lips to mine. I pushed her away, a little harder than I intended, sending her flying against the wall. "You don't love me! Not like that, anyway."

"But I do!" Mel exclaimed, seemingly unphased by the brute force I'd used to repel her advance.

I locked eyes with Mel again. "You don't *love me*. Not romantically."

"You saved me! You're my everything! And we're both vampires. We can be together forever. But there's just one thing. That Jinx. She has to go... I'll take care of—"

"Stop!" I screamed. The confusion on Mel's face told me everything I needed to know. Maybe my sire bond reset the cupid's magic. But now she'd fixed her obsession on *me.* And my sire bond wasn't going to fix it. Not this time.

"But I can't stand to exist without you!" Mel arched her fingers and slammed her hand against her chest, nails tearing through flesh.

"What are you doing!" I grabbed Mel's hands. "Stop this!"

"I'm ripping out my heart! If I can't be with you, Mercy, I don't want to live..."

I locked my eyes on Mel's. I didn't know if my sire bond could influence her at all given her condition but I had to try. And if that didn't work, well, at the very least I had to tell her something to stop her from hurting herself.

"You're right," I said. "Don't hurt yourself. We can be together. But let me handle things with Juliet. She's strong, Mel. I have to keep you here for your safety. I couldn't stand it if she realized how we felt about each other and tried to hurt you."

Mel's eyes watered up with false tears. "Mercy! I knew it! You do love me!"

I winced and forced myself to kiss her cheek. I'm a shitty actress. That was the best I could do. "Just give me some time, alright? I'll have some blood brought in for you, okay?"

Mel clapped her hands. "Thank you! I can't wait! We're going to get married. We're going to have little vampire babies together! Somehow!"

"Right," I cleared my throat. "Just be patient, Mel. I know it's hard. But it will be worth the wait."

I turned to leave.

"Mercy?"

I glanced back at my cupid-infected progeny. "Yeah, Mel?"

"Happy Valentine's Day!"

"Yeah, you too."

I left the cell and locked the door behind me. So much for fixing things with my sire bond. But at least Mel was safe. For the time being. But if the cupid's obsession was as powerful as I suspected, how long would she wait before the magic turned her suicidal again?

There was only one way I knew to end this. And we had to end it fast. We had to kill the cupids.

Chapter 3

STEPPING OUT OF MEL'S cell, my body was numb and emotionless. But I knew exactly what needed to be done. My mind remained logical and focused.

Suddenly, a high-pitched giggle pierced through the hallways, sending chills down my spine. It was that goddamn cupid. We had him locked up just two doors down from Mel's cell. How the hell did he escape?

With my wand at the ready, I sprinted toward the wicked laughter. Tracking down anything in the labyrinthine Underground was difficult without access to Mel's security system. And she was the only one of us who knew how to operate the damn thing.

Every time I hit an intersection in the halls, I had to stop and wait until the cupid made another noise. So far, I hadn't encountered a single member of our team.

Where the hell was everyone?

As I approached the throne room, I could hear a cacophony of sounds echoing through the stone walls. My heart raced with dread as I pushed open the heavy doors and was greeted by an unexpected sight—a dozen vampires, all completely naked. The overpowering scent of arousal filled the air as they frolicked around the room, the cupid's arrows flying in a chaotic display of pink magic that even Barbie would find excessive.

My eyes darted around the room, searching for Juliet, but she was nowhere to be found. Instead, two of her younglings were shamelessly doing the dirty *on my freaking throne.* On one of the velvet couches was a threesome, the fellow in the middle skewered from both ends like a shish kabob.

Just as I was about to call out for Juliet, I caught sight of a streak of pink light. Three of the cupid's arrows were flying straight at me. I dove out of the way, narrowly avoiding all three.

More giggles. The cupid was *amused,* reveling in lewd chaos.

I gritted my teeth and prepared for another attack as Antoine gyrated towards me with his manhood bouncing wildly. This was not how I had envisioned my night going when I set out on this mission.

"Juliet!" I called out desperately, hoping she would come to my aid. But she was still missing from the scene, leaving me to fend for myself against these oversexed and mischievous creatures.

But she was nowhere to be found. Where the hell was she?

All I knew was that if I couldn't take down the cupid fast, steal one of its arrows, and kill the little fucker, my entire team—apart from Juliet and me—was done for. It was only a matter of time before their lusts turned deadly.

Clement and the orphans weren't there. They lived in a wing removed from the primary base. So far as I knew, they were fine. But the orphans weren't trained to fight.

My best chance of ending this was to take down the cupid myself. I considered making a move towards him right then and there, but the gaze of a dozen debaucherous vampires stopped me in my tracks. Their red, lustful eyes were fixed on me. The cupid was using his arrows like a skilled artist, manipulating the victims' desires towards each other—and mostly towards me. His magic was still a mystery to me, but it was clear that if all these vampires were suddenly lusting after me, it would only lead to jealousy and chaos. I had no choice but to make a quick escape from the throne room before things spiraled out of control.

With one final desperate attempt, I aimed my wand at the menacing cupid before darting out of the room. *Enerva!*

But my efforts were in vain as the creature easily dodged the spell. In a panic, I activated a hand-sensor on the door, sealing it shut and trapping everyone inside my throne room.

For all I knew, the cupid would keep firing his arrows until my entire team killed each other. The only thing worse than that would be to let the little fucker out. I didn't have another choice.

I couldn't bother to think about worst-case scenarios. My priority was finding Juliet. She had to be somewhere in the facility. Why wasn't she with the others in that room? It didn't matter. All that mattered was getting her help, along with Clement and the orphans, if we had any chance of capturing the bloodthirsty cupid.

Frantically, I raced through the halls, shouting Juliet's name.

Silence echoed back at me.

After searching through the abandoned cells, I finally found Juliet in one of the rooms, curled up in a corner. Her gaze was fixed ahead, her expression unreadable.

"Juliet?"

She slowly lifted her head to look at me with narrowed eyes. "Hey."

"What happened? That cupid is causing chaos in my throne room along with the entire Underground!"

"I know."

I tilted my head. "You know?"

"He shot me with his arrow. He woke up and I didn't see it coming. And then I let him out. It's all my fault."

My heart twisted at her words. "He shot you with his arrow?"

Juliet nodded, a bitter laugh escaping her lips. "I should apologize. I messed up. That's what I should say. But honestly? I don't care."

I bit my lip, knowing exactly how she felt. "I understand."

"No, you don't! I feel absolutely nothing!"

I let out a heavy sigh. "I do understand."

"You don't get it, Mercy. It's not just that I don't care about the cupid, I don't feel a damn thing for you either."

I extended my hand. "The arrow affected me the same way."

Juliet grabbed my hand and while she didn't need my assistance, I helped her to her feet. "You don't understand. I haven't felt this way since…"

"Since you were with Jector? Since you terrorized London?"

Juliet shrugged her shoulders. "I felt something then. I relished in the kill. I enjoyed it. Now, though. I just feel…"

"Cold and dead?"

Juliet stared at me blankly for a few moments before nodding curtly. "I know I should care, but…"

"You feel zero emotion. It's like the cupid's arrow interacted with us differently than everyone else. I think it interacted with our blood bond and the passion we had for each other and the cupid's magic canceled the other out."

"Interesting theory. But you know what?"

"You still don't give a shit?"

Juliet scratched the back of her head. "Right."

"But we still have our memories. We know what we felt before. I remember feeling happy."

Juliet took a deep breath and released it through flapping lips. "Yeah. Me too."

"Objectively speaking, I know that if I stay numb for long, I'll do some shit that will haunt me later. If I ever get my emotions back, I'll regret it."

Juliet furrowed her brow. "Yeah, all true. Thing is, I *still* don't give a flying fuck."

I furrowed my brow. "A flying fuck? That sounds like an incredibly difficult maneuver."

Juliet smirked. "It does, doesn't it?"

I pursed my lips. "I'm with you. I want nothing more than to do nothing at all right now. But I know deep down that doing nothing will only leave me numb like this forever. If I feel anything right now, it's that I wish I felt something."

Juliet leaned against the wall and crossed her arms. "Well, this isn't *all* bad."

I shook my head. "We can't use our lack of emotions to justify going on a binge, Juliet."

"Please," Juliet rolled her eyes. "Give me some credit. That's not what I'm suggesting."

I shrugged. "Then what?"

"If our blood bond can impact how a cupid's magic works, that means there's something in blood that we might be able to use against the cupid other than its own arrows."

I cocked an eyebrow. "Juliet, we can't forge a blood bond with every vampire in the underground. I mean, we could, but that could only make things worse. And it would be hard to do given everyone's present condition."

"That's not what I'm suggesting. You're a witch, right? As a vampire, you can access the power that's latent in blood."

I sighed. "I try not to. There's only one witch I've ever known who has dealt in bloodwitchery and didn't destroy herself in the process."

"That vampire you raised back in New Orleans?" Juliet asked.

I nodded. "Hailey Bradbury. She's still a young vampire, but she's one hell of a witch. If anyone knows how to deal with this shit, it's her."

Chapter 4

I made the call. Two minutes later, a multicolored flash filled the small cell where Juliet and I waited.

"Pauli's here, bitches!" the rainbow colored boa-constrictor announced while draped over Hailey's shoulders.

We didn't have time to waste. Hailey didn't have teleportation abilities. Pauli did. Pauli was a hougan—a voodoo priest with the aspect of Aida Wedo, the Loa of snakes and rainbows. He could shape-shift between his serpentine and human forms. As a snake, he could travel pretty much anywhere around the world. So long as he knew where he was going, and could visualize it, he could get there.

Pauli was also an acquired taste. His flamboyance was over the top. That wasn't the issue. I *love* flamboyant men. They can be a hell of a lot of fun. That wasn't Pauli's problem.

He wasn't just flamboyant. He was downright obscene. As long as I'd known Pauli, he took every chance he had to flaunt his oversized manhood—which he'd enhanced with his shapeshifting abilities to absurd proportions. I mean, don't get me wrong. Most men are obsessed with their own genitals. Pauli *revered* his.

It was as if he thought his dick was a divine relic and by showing it off, granting others the privilege to gaze upon its obscene girth, he was doing people a favor. Blessing them beyond measure—and it was *certainly* beyond measure.

Pauli and I also had a history. Not of the romantic sort. I wasn't his type, to say the least. But I'd bitten him a time or two. On the *neck*. Just in case *that* wasn't clear.

No hard feelings. Because he didn't have *hard* feelings for women.

We tolerated one another. Bygones and whatnot. And I had to admit, it took balls—not just a shaft—to bring Hailey to the Underground. He wasn't a vampire, after all. He was like a juicy steak dropped into a lion's den. We had a few younglings, now warped by the cupid, who'd be more than happy to take a bite... especially if he didn't put that *thing* away.

But he was only here because we needed him to get Hailey to us as quickly as possible. So far as I was concerned, he could leave at any time. Then again, his shifting and teleportation abilities could come in handy. Especially since Muggs was compromised.

Hailey was looking cute as ever. She was a natural-born witch, inheriting her abilities from the infamous Moll Dyer. The same Moll, in fact, who'd first tutored me in the craft when I was just a girl living in Exeter.

While Hailey was now in her mid-twenties (human and vampire years combined) she became a vampire at sixteen. She looked more innocent than she was. No one would think she was, arguably, the most powerful witch in the world. Probably the most naturally talented witch in a century. While I always struggled to tap into the power latent in blood, a power I could access as a witch-turned-vampire, she embraced bloodwitchery wholesale.

Juliet tilted her head. "You're the badass blood witch I've heard so much about?"

Hailey shrugged. "I don't know. Mercy, you've been talking about me? I'm touched!"

I grinned. "Hailey might not be my progeny, but she's my protégé. Though I can't claim full responsibility for what she can do."

Pauli slithered down Haileys frame and, from a coiled position on the floor, shifted into a very naked human form. "I'm just here for the orgy."

I rolled my eyes. "Of course you are. But trust me, Pauli, this isn't anything like what you usually take part in on Friday nights."

"Friday nights have nothing on Wednesdays, honey."

Juliet furrowed her brow. "Wednesday? Who has *fun* on Wednesdays?"

"Hump day!!!" Pauli exclaimed. "Why do you think they call it that, anyway? Believe you me. Camels have nothing to do with it."

Hailey snickered and nudged Pauli in his bony ribs. "The difference is that it will not be fun—at all. I've never encountered a cupid before, but if its arrows somehow interact with blood, I might be able to devise a spell that can nullify its effects. Since you two were both hit by the cupid's arrows and weren't affected the same as other vampires, it must have to do with something you two have in common that none of the other victims do."

"We had a blood bond before," I added. "That's the only thing we can think of as to why the arrow didn't affect us like it did everyone else."

Hailey nodded. "I've had my share of experiences with blood bonds. An obsession that can be forged in a bond like that isn't that different from what you're explaining happened to those attacked by the cupids."

Juliet shook her head. "It was different for us. Mercy and I weren't obsessed. We loved each other."

"You thought you did," Hailey added without a moment's pause. "And maybe you really did. But a person—even a vampire—can't handle too many different kinds of love magic working at once. Think of it like drinking a pot of coffee, followed by a case of Red Bull. Eventually, the mind is so overwhelmed by the caffeine that it takes a toll and you feel less a surge of energy or focus and instead are so distracted by the jitters it's counterproductive."

"You think that's what happened to us?" I asked. "I figured the blood bond and the cupid's magic probably canceled each other out."

"I don't think that's likely," Hailey said. "Any kind of love magic has to manipulate hormones, the brain itself. Flood the mind with too many stimuli and it doesn't know how to respond. It shuts down the emotions completely."

"But we're vampires, "Juliet added. "Aren't we more resistant to shit like that than humans?"

"In this case?" Hailey shook her head. "It's actually the opposite. Any kind of magic that enters a person through blood will actually affect a vampire more profoundly than it does a mortal."

"Because we metabolize blood regularly?" I pinched my chin.

Hailey nodded. "Precisely. And since vampires can actually absorb or metabolize magical properties within blood that usually remain dormant in ninety-nine percent of humans, the impact is far less predictable."

I grabbed Juliet's hand. I hoped I'd feel something when I did, but my emotions remained numb. "Are you saying this will wear off?"

Hailey winced. "It's hard to say. I see a few possibilities. I don't think this situation will last as it is. Eventually, things will change. The body will adapt. Your body will either maintain the blood bond you feel for each other, or it will discard it in favor of the cupid's magic."

"That's only two possibilities," Juliet said. "You said you think there are a few. What else could happen?"

Hailey sighed. "Your minds are overwhelmed. The condition could drive you mad. Or, perhaps worse, the cupid's magic might need to find some other receptor in the brain to attach itself to. Rather than stoking your passions, the magic might adapt and trigger something else."

"Something else?" I tilted my head.

"Intense sadness. Unrestrained rage. Uncontrollable giddiness. There's no telling what could happen."

"So using us like some kind of host animal with resistance to create a magical vaccine is off the table?" Juliet asked.

Hailey nodded. "It doesn't work that way. I wish it did. It's going to get worse before it gets better. For both of you."

I cleared my throat. "Muggs said that if we kill the cupid who shot us, it'll dispel the creature's magic. Sounds to me like we're back to Plan A. The only way to really beat this thing is to kill the cupids."

"Wait," Pauli added. "There's more than one?"

"We've seen four of them, at least. The one that shot me is somewhere downtown."

"But the cupid that shot me," Juliet added, "is still in the throne room with the rest of the team."

"Then that's where we start." Hailey pulled her wand out from a custom pocket sewn into her jeans. "Between the four of us, we stand a decent chance. Is there anyone else who can help?"

I bit my lip. "Only Clement and the vampire orphans. I'd rather not put anyone else at risk, though, if we can avoid it."

"We might not have a choice," Hailey said. "Our best chance against the cupid will be to separate it from the other vampires who it can manipulate and influence. The more it's surrounded by chaos, the greater its advantage. We could use some help to pull the other vampires out of that room so that we can take on the cupid four against one."

I nodded. "Alright. That's a plan. But Pauli? We need to get you some goddamn clothes. Because if you get struck by a cupid's arrow like that… well…"

"I know!" Pauli added. "I could poke someone's eye out with this thing!"

Chapter 5

I gave Pauli directions to Ladinas's old room so he could find something to wear. He must've made a wrong turn because when Hailey, Juliet and I met back up with him he was wearing one of *my* Victorian dresses.

"God damn it, Pauli."

He smirked at me. "You know the difference between you and me, honey?"

I snorted. "I already know what you're going to say."

"I make this dress look good!"

Juliet bit her lip. "I beg to differ. But whatever."

Pauli extended his open palm toward Juliet. "Talk to the hand."

Juliet smirked. "Wow. So, you can teleport. You can also time travel?"

Pauli furrowed his brow. "No. I can't do that."

"Because I just had a flashback, and it was the nineteen nineties. People don't say 'talk to the hand' anymore. And that quote, about making the dress look good? That was *Men in Black*."

"Well, you better talk to this hand, bitch! Cuz the face ain't listening!"

Juliet hissed, exposing her fangs. "What the fuck did you just call me?"

Hailey sighed and put her hand on Juliet's shoulder. "Don't take it personally. Pauli calls *everyone* a bitch."

I grabbed Juliet's arm. "Hold on. Did that actually anger you when he called you a bitch?"

Juliet tilted her head. "You're right. I felt something. But it's not love. More like low-key rage."

"Low key?" Pauli giggled. "You're giving me shit for summoning the nineties? You're a two-hundred year old vampire and you're talking like you belong to Gen Z. How *sus* is that?"

"Shut up, Pauli," I interjected. "The point is that Juliet felt an emotion."

Hailey sighed and fixed her eyes on Juliet. "I'm not sure that's a good thing. It means the cupid's magic is looking for a place to take hold in your mind. Don't entertain your anger at all. Doing that will open the floodgates to the magic. It'll consume you."

I sighed. "The last thing we need is a vampire full-on pissed off at everything and everyone with the same intensity that usually results in unrestrained lust."

Juliet gulped. "I'd be like Jector…"

I nodded. "And the last thing we need is Juliet the Ripper on the loose in Providence."

"Like I said," Hailey interrupted, "we need to stop the cupid that's here. If we can catch that thing quickly, Juliet will be fine."

Enough shooting the shit. If Juliet was already showing symptoms it was only a matter of time before things got worse. I was shot before she was. Why wasn't I showing symptoms already? Probably because I was a witch. I had a tolerance for magic that a muggle like Juliet didn't.

That didn't mean shit wouldn't hit the fan sooner or later.

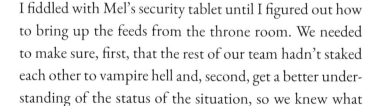

I fiddled with Mel's security tablet until I figured out how to bring up the feeds from the throne room. We needed to make sure, first, that the rest of our team hadn't staked each other to vampire hell and, second, get a better understanding of the status of the situation, so we knew what we were heading into.

The throne room, once a place of regal darkness and whispered conspiracies, now resembled a Roman bathhouse. The scene was lewd, shocking, and... *sticky*. Enough to make Larry Flint blush.

We stood at the threshold, my hellhound at my side. We needed all hands—and paws—on deck if we were going to pull this off. Clement, Ian, and a gaggle of orphan vamps filtered into the hall behind us.

"We're here to help," Clement suggested. "But this isn't going to be easy. We need a plan."

"I have an idea," Juliet nodded, her piercings reflecting dim security lights. "I can influence the younglings. They'll heed my command, I think. Just like with a sire bond. They'll follow me if I can get through to them."

"Jinx," I sighed, "when I used my sire bond on Mel, she ended up wanting to hump my leg like an un-neutered Pomeranian. It's too much of a risk. If the same thing happens and *all* the younglings fix their lusts on you..."

"I think it's the best chance we have," Hailey interrupted. "You can't distract someone from a magical compulsion with treats. It's going to take something equally powerful to lure them out of there. The bond that Juliet has with the younglings might be the only chance we have to pull this off."

I grunted. "I don't know. Juliet struts in there, plays Pied Piper. The rest won't follow because they like the sound of her tune. They're going to want one thing, and subjecting Juliet to *that*..."

Juliet shook her head. "I'll be fine. I'm faster and older than any of the younglings. Let them come after me. If I can bend their lusts toward me, at least we'll be able to lure them where we want. It'll give us *some* semblance of control over the team. And if all goes according to plan, the web of desire will tangle up the rest of the Underground vampires at the same time. It's the only way we're going to get all of them out of there. It's the only chance we have to corner that cupid without their interference."

I scratched the back of my head. "Juliet, I don't know..."

"Look." Juliet clenched her fists. "That cupid *shot* me. The rage is building by the second. This might be our only chance to deal with this before it overwhelms me. I'm already compromised. But while I still have some semblance of my wits about me, we have to take advantage of this chance."

If I still had my affections intact, I might not have agreed. My protest against the plan was mostly *intellectual*. But her argument was sound. I didn't have a better plan, and since Hailey was on board with it and I trusted her judgment, I reluctantly agreed. "Alright. If this doesn't work, you bail. Get the hell out of here. Let us deal with the infected."

"Scout's honor," Juliet replied with a half-cocked grin. "Not that I'm a scout, or have much honor at all. But you can trust me. I'm not in the mood for a gang bang."

Pauli snickered. "Gang bangs and Boy Scouts. Those were the days…"

I rolled my eyes. I really hoped Pauli made that up. But then again, it was Pauli. You never knew for sure.

"Alright, everyone, eyes sharp and fangs sharper," I barked, my voice echoing slightly in the dimly lit corridor. "Clement, you and the orphans form a perimeter. Once Juliet lures everyone out here, it's going to be a frenzy. Shield her any way you can, but if the cupid gets out, run. Don't take any risks. We don't need more love-struck vampires."

Clement rolled up his sleeves. "We'll keep her safe, Mercy. You have my word." The orphans, a motley crew of fledgling vampires with more courage than common sense, nodded in unison, their expressions determined.

"Good. Keep it tight. No heroics," I warned, but I knew they'd do whatever it took. They had that look in their eyes—the same one I saw in the mirror every time shit soiled my Sunday.

I turned to face the throne room door and pressed my hand against the palm reader mounted on the wall. The security locks disengaged with a series of clicks and hisses.

Juliet gave me a curt nod. "Time to play bait."

"Remember, get out if it goes pear-shaped," I said, but the doors were already closing behind her.

"Pauli, Hailey, Goliath—positions." I glanced back at my team. Goliath growled low in his throat. Pauli, with all the subtlety of a circus clown at a funeral, winked at me, while Hailey cracked her knuckles, looking far too excited for someone about to wrangle a creature that could turn this whole skirmish into an orgy with a flick of its wrist.

"Mercy, when this is over, we're definitely getting drunk," Hailey whispered, and I couldn't help but smirk.

"Good luck with that. Vampires can't *get* drunk."

Hailey shrugged. "I know a spell. I can make it happen."

I tightened my grip on my wand. "I'll hold you to that."

The throne room doors burst open, a swarm of naked vampires gyrating on top of each other like maggots on a three-week old donut. Juliet didn't hesitate. She slipped through the door and barked out orders. One-by-one the younglings separated themselves from the pile.

So far—everything was going according to plan.

"In position!" I shouted, and Clement and the orphans sprang into action, forming a barrier in the hallway. Juliet took off with impressive speed. The younglings followed behind her, arms flailing, boners and breasts bouncing.

It was working. The younglings were fixated on her, following her every move, giving us the opening we needed. It didn't take long before Antoine and the rest of the original team followed, equally dazed by desire.

"Keep them busy," I said, then motioned to Hailey and Pauli. "Now!" We dashed into the throne room, Goliath on my heels. The plan was simple: find the cupid, immobilize it, and stake the fucker with its own arrow. Do that, and we'd get Juliet and the rest of the team back. We'd have a chance to take on the other cupids still on the loose. We could save Muggs and Mel.

"Where are you, you little winged freak?" I muttered under my breath, scanning the opulent room for any sign of our diminutive adversary. It had to be here, somewhere among the velvet drapes and gilded furnishings.

"Split up! And watch for arrows," I commanded. "It's in here somewhere."

The curtains fluttered.

Gotcha. "*Enerva!*"

The spell shot from the tip of my wand. The little bastard flew out from behind the curtains, narrowly escaping my magic.

"Damn it!"

"I've got this." Hailey had her own wand ready. She traced it through the air, an intricate pattern that corresponded with a spell I'd never learned. Whatever she was up to, I trusted it would do the job. Hailey's magic was unique. Nothing you're likely to learn from a common grimoire or a coven. Most of what she could do followed from her *own* experimentation.

A series of crimson glyphs formed on the ceiling. "Try to chase it into one of my traps!"

I didn't question the method. If these symbols could contain a cupid, it was worth a try. However, as the symbols shifted and formed vertical barriers, creating an intricate maze of traps, the cupid maneuvered through them with unexpected agility.

"Come on, you little shit!" I spat, but the cupid seemed almost drunk on its own mischief, ducking and weaving through our spells with infuriating grace, firing arrows at us with an impressive precision.

We evaded, leapt, and tumbled to avoid the onslaught of cupid's arrows. How was that tiny menace able to shoot at us so damn accurately while also dodging our spells?

"Mercy! Behind you!" Pauli's warning came just in time, and I twisted to see an arrow whiz past where my head had been a split second earlier.

As if in slow motion, I helplessly witnessed the arrow hurtle towards Goliath. With a guttural cry, I desperately yelled out a warning to him, but it was already too late. The sharp projectile found its target, lodging itself deep in Goliath's side. His majestic body quivered with a mix of pain and determination, his dark fur absorbing the impact like a shield.

"Shit," I hissed, expecting him to succumb to the charm any moment, to turn into another love struck puppet. But Goliath merely shook his massive frame, growled low in his throat, and sniffed at the air.

Crisis averted. Maybe? For now.

"Pauli!" Hailey shouted, her voice a pitch higher than usual, betraying her concern. "We need that quiver!"

With a multi-colored streak of light trailing behind him, he leapt into the air off Hailey's shoulders—or teleported; with Pauli, it was hard to tell the difference—and reappeared mid-flight, jaws agape. The cupid, caught off guard for once, let out a squawk of surprise as a set of fanged jaws snatched the quiver from its back.

"You just got Pauli'd, bitch!"

The cupid gyrated, its pudgy arms flailed. A futile attempt to cling to its quiver. Pauli was too fast. He curled his luminescent body, but the move allowed the cupid to slip free. At least Pauli had the quiver. We still needed to *catch* the little fucker.

Pauli teleported back to Hailey's shoulders, the cupid's quiver dangling from his coils.

"Mercy, grab one. It's time we flipped the script!" Hailey retrieved an arrow from the quiver. Her face shifted when she touched it. "This is... unique."

I plucked a single arrow from the quiver with a reverence I didn't feel. The shaft was warm to the touch, thrumming with an energy that made my skin prickle. "Whatever. We have arrows. Now to give the cupid a taste of its own bullshit."

Hailey nodded. "We have to catch it first."

"On it!" Pauli announced, teleporting off Hailey's shoulders again, leaving the quiver dangling from Hailey's arm.

Now that the cupid knew what Pauli could do, though, it was ready. One colorful flash after the next, Pauli appeared, disappeared, and reappeared in rapid succession, always just a beat late.

"Come to Pauli, you little shit!"

Hailey and I took off, using our speed to hem the little bugger in. If we could force the cupid to pause mid-flight for a split second, Pauli might be able to catch it.

Even with our strength and speed, which exceeded the cupid's, he had the advantage of flight. We could jump and reach him anywhere, but we couldn't alter our course mid-leap.

To make matters worse, the floor was slicker than snot. But *snot* wasn't the particular bodily fluid that was smeared across the marble tile... ugh...

"Damn vampire semen!" Hailey screamed as her feet slipped, nearly forcing her to do the splits.

Just then, the doors burst open, and Juliet stormed in, her eyes narrow and jaw tight.

"Juliet?" I called out, taken aback by the raw anger etched on her usually composed face.

"Stay out of my way, Mercy," she spat, marching into the fray. Her fists clenched and unclenched, itching for a fight.

"Jinx, what are you—"

"Going to smash that flying rat into oblivion," she seethed.

"Great," I muttered under my breath. "Because things weren't chaotic enough."

I exchanged a quick glance with Hailey. This was what we were afraid of. The cupid's magic had activated Juliet's rage rather than her lust. But if she could channel that anger to drop the cupid, we could kill it before her condition worsened.

Meanwhile, as Juliet's vendetta unfolded with the grace of a hurricane, Pauli chose that moment to revert to his human form. "It's no use. I'm spent. We need another plan."

I was inclined to let Juliet do her worst. She was every bit as fast as I was. And if her magically induced fury gave her an edge, who was I to get in her way? For now, at least, the cupid was stuck in the throne room. We'd catch the little shit, eventually.

But as Pauli stood there in all his unclothed glory, an unusual howl sounded behind us.

Goliath was breathing heavily. His eyes were glossed over and fixed on Pauli.

He wasn't immune to the cupid's magic, after all.

"Uh-oh," Pauli muttered, catching sight of Goliath's love-struck gaze. "This isn't good."

"Run!" I yelled, as Goliath began advancing toward him with all the subtlety of a freight train.

"Seriously?" Pauli groaned, before taking off at a sprint. "I'm not your type, big guy!"

"Try telling him that," I said dryly, watching the two of them circle around the room.

"Can we focus, please?" Hailey interjected, ducking as a couch flew past her. Juliet had tried to throw the damn thing at the cupid and didn't seem to notice we were standing in the way.

"Juliet!" I screamed. "Watch it!"

She was blinded by rage. I wasn't sure she even noticed we were in the room. All she could think about was eviscerating the cupid.

"Down boy!" Pauli shrieked.

"Damn it, teleport away from him!" I shouted.

"Don't you think I would if I could?" Pauli grunted. "I've spent all my magic trying to chase down that little bitch. I need to recharge!"

Between Juliet turning into the hulk, and Goliath horny for Pauli, the chaos was too much. I glanced at Hailey. "What the hell are we going to do now?"

"Kill the cupid, all this ends. Don't lose focus, Mercy!"

But Pauli was streaking past us, and with an aroused Goliath pursuing him, I lost it.

A giggle escaped my lips. I *never* giggled, but I couldn't stop it. I mean, there was something humorous about Pauli getting his comeuppance, courtesy of a hellhound. But this was something else…

"Mercy!" Hailey screamed. "Get your shit together! This is the cupid's doing."

She was right. Our blood bond prevented the cupid's magic from turning Juliet and me into passion possessed bloodsuckers, but the magic was finding different ways to affect our emotions.

Juliet was filled with rage. I was consumed with… *hilarity*.

"Hey Pauli!" I snorted through my words, unable to suppress my laughter. "I thought you *liked* doing it doggy!"

"Fuck you!" Pauli shouted back.

I *lost* it. For some reason, being f-bombed by a terrified Pauli was the funniest thing I ever heard.

The next thing I knew, I was rolling around in whatever bodily fluids still coated the marble floor, slamming my fist against the ground and unable to contain my chortles.

Hailey took a step back, her eyes wide as saucers. "Mercy, snap out of it! Juliet's the only one trying to kill the cupid and we have to help her! I don't trust her with the arrows. We need to do it now!"

"Gah, Hailey!" I screeched, wiping tears from my eyes. "You want to *do it* with me? Are you sure you didn't accidentally stick yourself with an arrow?"

"Stop it, Mercy!" Hailey insisted.

"I can't! It's all so goddamn funny! I'm laughing so hard I can't concentrate!"

Hailey, seeing my compelled state, crossed her arms and sighed. "I've got an idea. But it won't solve the problem, and it's going to hurt like hell. It might make things worse after it wears off."

"What's the idea?" I asked, trying to regain my composure to no avail. Goliath was still in heat and Pauli remained his object of lust. The whole thing was just so damn funny. "Do what you have to do! Muuuuahahaha!"

Hailey muttered something under her breath. I was laughing so hard I couldn't make out her words. But the next thing I knew, something hit me—a spell of some kind, and for a brief moment, a searing heat bubbled in my veins. "Shit!" I screamed, "I'm boiling! Make it stop!"

She didn't stop. She maintained her spell until the pain subsided. I still *wanted* to laugh. Whatever she did, it gave me enough focus that I could return to my feet. "What the hell was that?"

"Blood magic," Hailey explained. "I basically focused dormant energy within your blood and burned out the part of your brain that's affected. I don't think I got it all. And since you're a vampire, you'll heal and probably be worse off when it's done. But it gives us a chance to take out this cupid."

I nodded. "We better hurry. Because the cupid that shot *me* is still out there somewhere. And we're going to need to find it before I'm reduced to laughing fits again."

"Can you call off your hellhound?" Hailey asked.

I bit my lip. "I can try. Goliath!"

The hellhound paused for a split second, panting. But he just as quickly returned his focus to Pauli.

I shook my head. "Not going to work."

"Ever hear of consent, you motherfucker?" Pauli screamed. "Hurry, damn it! Kill that cupid!"

I grinned a little, but Hailey's magic was working for now. I resisted the urge to fall into stitches and grabbed my wand.

"Juliet!" I shouted. "Corner him! I'll drop him!"

She didn't hear me. But she was so damn determined to catch the cupid that it worked out.

I aimed my wand at the cupid, my laughter now stifled by determination. As Hailey chanted a spell to prepare for her own attack, I focused on the cupid's erratic movements, trying to time my shot perfectly. Juliet was closing in fast, her eyes burning with fury.

Just as the cupid turned to flee, it froze mid-stride. My "enerva" spell had successfully immobilized it. I grinned triumphantly as Juliet lunged forward, snatching an arrow from the quiver hanging on Hailey's shoulder.

With a swift motion, Juliet plunged the arrow into the cupid's chest. "Die! Die! Die!"

A burst of light erupted from the wound, and in an instant, the cupid disintegrated into ash. The room fell silent except for my ragged breaths and the crackling of the dying embers.

I looked at Juliet in awe. The rage that had consumed her moments ago was replaced with a mix of relief and exhaustion. She dropped to her knees, tears streaming down her cheeks.

Goliath whimpered and nuzzled my side. Pauli sighed in relief.

"Well, that was... entertaining," I said, trying to regain my composure. "But we have a job to do."

Hailey nodded. "One down. How many of these little bastards did you say are still out there?"

"We saw at least three more," Juliet added, resting her hand on my shoulder. I resisted the urge to shrug off her affectionate touch. "Are you okay, Mercy?"

"I don't know. I don't have a lot of time. We have to find the cupid that shot me and kill it. Not to mention the cupid that shot Mel and Muggs."

Juliet cleared her throat. "Don't forget about Alice."

I nodded. "Right. We have to save Alice, too."

Meanwhile, Pauli was wincing in pain. "What's wrong?" Hailey asked.

"Anal cramps!" Pauli huffed. "I was clenching so hard, afraid your dog was going to make me his bitch. I think I pulled my sphincter."

"You can *pull* your sphincter?" I tilted my head and cocked my left eyebrow. "Never mind. I don't need to know."

Chapter 6

The silence was deafening. I stood in the hallway, surveying the awkward scene before me. The Underground's vampires were all stripped bare, avoiding each other's gazes as they shuffled about self-consciously. A few of them had their gangly bits tucked between their legs, some of them cupped their junk in one hand. Still others remained turned to the wall—each butt like a bad moon rising.

I cleared my throat, channeling my irritation into authority. "Alright, listen up. I know we're all feeling a little... embarrassed. But we need to get our shit together if we're going to take down the other cupids and save our people."

I paused, meeting the eyes of each vampire in turn. Most looked away, but a few held my gaze.

"I'm not going to lie. Things look bad. Mel, Muggs, and Alice are still infected, and we have no idea how much chaos those fuckers have unleashed on the surface. But we can't give up hope." My voice hardened. "We've taken out one of those winged freaks. We can kill the others too if we work together. But that means swallowing your pride and moving past this."

I gestured to Clement and Jinx. "You two start getting people dressed and back to their senses. The rest of you—" I broke off, distracted by a glimpse of Antoine out of the corner of my eye.

I couldn't help it. A wave of uncontrollable laughter overcame me as I stared at his pathetically tiny package. I doubled over, clutching my stomach.

"Oh... oh god," I wheezed between fits of hysterics. "You're hung like a horse... fly! Get it, hung like a horse fly!"

Antoine quickly turned away, cupping himself.

Still shaking with mirth, I felt a hand on my shoulder. Hailey. Her expression was stern.

"Get it together, Mercy," she muttered under her breath. "The cupid's magic is making you act this way. Fight it."

I wiped a tear from my eye, letting out a final chuckle. "Yeah, yeah. You're right. It's just so damn hard." I smirked. "A stiff inch and a quarter!"

Hailey rolled her eyes and grabbed my arm. "Come on, let's go check on Mel." Pauli, draped around her neck in snake form, bobbed his rainbow-hued head in agreement.

As we headed down the hall, I shook my head, trying to focus. Hailey was right. Her spell was the only thing stopping me from descending into unrestrained laughter. I had to get my head in the game. Something I imagined Antoine found difficult to do because... well... he would come up short!

I took a deep breath. Antoine's condition wasn't a comedy. It was a *tragedy*. For anyone who might become his lover.

We arrived at Mel's cell, only to find the heavy iron door ripped from its hinges. Mel was gone.

"Shit!" I hissed, scanning the dark hallway for any sign of her. Where could she have gone? And why? She was under the influence of the cupid's spell, obsessed with me. What was her plan?

A blood-curdling scream echoed down the corridor. I exchanged a worried glance with Hailey before taking off at vampire speed, following the sound. Mel couldn't have gotten far.

Skidding around a corner, I caught sight of her silhouette up ahead. Even in the dim light, I could see she was holding something—a pointed stake. My dead heart dropped. This was bad.

"Mel!" I called out. She turned, eyes widening at my sudden appearance.

"Mercy!" A delirious smile spread across her face. "I knew you'd find me."

I approached cautiously. "What are you doing with that stake, Mel?"

She glanced down at the bloodied tip. "Oh, this? Don't worry about it, my love. I took care of everything."

My throat went dry. She wouldn't... would she?

"Please," I whispered. "Tell me you didn't..."

Mel stepped closer, an unsettling gleam in her eye.

"I staked Juliet. Now we can finally be together."

I stared at Mel in horror, unable to process her words at first. She *staked* Juliet?

"Why?" I finally choked out, even though I knew the answer. The cupid's magic made Mel think she loved me—and this was the inevitable result.

Mel tilted her head, frowning slightly, as if the answer should be obvious. "For us, my darling. With Juliet out of the way, we can be together freely. Just you and me."

I felt sick. The cupid's spell had warped Mel's mind completely, filling her with a twisted obsession. This wasn't the resourceful vampire I knew and respected. And she wasn't into women, last I checked. Then again, neither was I before Juliet and I shared a blood bond.

"Mel," I whispered. "You're not thinking clearly. The cupid's magic is clouding your judgment."

She shook her head stubbornly. "My love is real. I had to remove the obstacle to our happiness."

By this time, Hailey and Pauli had caught up to us. I turned to them desperately.

"Can you deal with her? I have to check on Juliet."

Hailey nodded, her youthful face grim. She started toward Mel slowly.

I didn't hesitate. Whirling around, I sprinted back the way I'd come. Rounding a corner, I skidded to a halt at the sight before me.

There was Juliet, staked viciously through the heart. Her body lay limp and gray in the middle of the hallway, the crowd of naked vampires surrounding her apathetic. What the hell? I turned to Clement.

"How could you let this happen? Mel is only a few years a vampire. You're one of the oldest vampires in the Underground!"

Clement sighed. "I didn't see it coming. I'm sorry. But Mel didn't burn out her heart. All is not lost."

He was right. While I could revive a staked vampire, a staking sends a vampire's spirit to hell. On a different plane of existence, a few minutes staked could feel like a year or longer. Then again, the time could pass in the blink of an eye. And many staked vampires came back traumatized. I could only hope Juliet was resilient enough to handle whatever hell threw at her.

Falling to my knees beside Juliet, I wrapped both hands around the stake's handle and pulled with all my strength. It came free with a sickening squelch. Juliet's eyes flew open, clouded with pain and confusion. I cradled her gently, whispering words of comfort as her wound slowly knitted back together.

I wasn't mad at Mel. Partially because most of my emotions remained dormant. But I also know it wasn't her fault. It was the cupid's chaos that had caused this. Mel still thought of Juliet as my girlfriend. While I didn't feel a thing for Juliet at the moment, I remembered what it felt like when I did. Enough to realize I hoped it was still possible to rekindle our romance when all this was over.

Juliet's eyes slowly focused on me, though she still seemed dazed.

"Mercy?" she croaked, her voice rough. "What... what happened?"

"You were staked," I breathed. "But you're back now."

Juliet's hand went to her chest, feeling the tender skin that was still knitting itself back together. Understanding dawned in her eyes.

"Mel..." she said. "She was out of her mind. The cupid..."

"I know," I said. "It's not her fault. But right now, you need to feed. You were in vampire hell. Let's get you some blood to get your strength back."

Juliet sighed. "Hell. It sort of sucks, you know."

I did my best to suppress my laughter. "That's why they call it hell. Are you going to be alright?"

Juliet cocked her head. "I think so... but I still feel..."

"Dead? Emotionless?"

Juliet nodded. "But when I saw you, for a split-second, I felt... I don't know. *Safe.*"

"Well, that's something." I helped Juliet to her feet slowly. She leaned heavily against me, still unsteady. As we walked down the hall, the other vampires watched us passively, showing no reaction. Their apathy was going to be a problem.

"Hey!" I shouted at them. "What the hell is wrong with you people?"

Antoine just shrugged, not meeting my eyes. "We didn't think it was a big deal," he mumbled. "We have our own issues right now..."

That's when I understood. The cupid's spell had left them wallowing in shame and melancholy. They were too lost in their own funk to care about anything else. I had to snap them out of it. But that might not be possible until we killed the cupid.

"Look..." I scratched the back of my head. "I don't feel much right now, either. But all our memories are there. We need to cling to what we know is right. I don't care if all you want to do is stand around with nothing but your dicks in your hands. You *remember* what we're about, we have a job to do, and we can't let these cupids get away with this shitshow."

"Understood," Antoine nodded. "We'll get dressed. One foot in front of the other. Do what we know is right, no matter what."

"You all need to move past this," I said firmly. "The cupid is dead, but the fight isn't over. We have a job to do. I'm taking Juliet up top to feed. When I get back, you better be ready for battle."

With that, I guided Juliet away. We had to keep moving.

Juliet leaned against me as we made our way to the elevator to the surface. She was still disoriented from the staking and subsequent trip to vampire hell.

"Just hold on, Jinx," I told her. "We'll get you fed and back on your feet in no time."

She gave me a wan smile. "Thanks, Mercy. Don't know what I'd do without you."

We emerged into the chilly night air. The Underground wasn't in the busiest part of town, but there were a few nearby bars. I tried not to use them to "hunt" more often than necessary. When vampires frequent the same haunts too often, it can rouse suspicion. But we didn't have time to waste.

Juliet and I entered a bar—little more than a hole-in-the wall, but it would do. I spotted a drunk businessman tipping back a shot at the bar. He was dressed like a cast member of *Suits*. Clean cut, a three-piece that cost more than some people made in a month. Why would someone so well-to-do hide out in a blue-collar bar? Because he didn't want anyone in his circle of urban professionals to recognize him. He wanted to entertain a binge without interference. Or he was hoping to pick up a cheap thrill. Either way, he was the perfect prey.

Not only was he likely at the bar *alone*. He was likely overindulging. The more intoxicated someone was, the easier it was to make them forget our encounter.

"Wait here," I told Juliet, the door closing behind us.

I approached the bar, my eyes scanning the room for anyone who might recognize me. After the episode with Oblivion, I was still a "wanted woman" among the authorities. It wasn't like they could do a damn thing if they caught me, but I also wasn't in the mood to deal with any bullshit. And without much emotion at all, well, I wasn't sure I could resist my primal urges if someone came at me with any aggression.

"Hey there," I purred, flashing my most charming smile at the tipsy executive. "Care to offer a lady a drink?"

He looked up, his bleary eyes widening as he took in my pale complexion and piercing gaze.

"I- uh, sure," he stammered, gesturing to the bartender. "What can I get you?"

The man clearly didn't know what *kind* of drink I was looking for. But I'd done this thousands of times. You can't go straight for the jugular until the prey is fully enthralled.

I ordered a whiskey on the rocks and glanced back at Juliet. She was still by the entrance, leaning against a wall with a weary expression on her face. I needed to lure this man someplace more private. It wouldn't take long. My allure was undeniable. Every vampire had the ability—but I'd always been especially *skilled* at baiting my male prey.

As I sipped the whiskey, I engaged in small talk with the businessman, skillfully guiding the conversation to a more intimate tone. He was putty in my hands, completely entranced by my charm. After a few minutes of flirting, I leaned in closer, lowering my voice to a seductive whisper.

"You know," I said, my lips grazing against his earlobe. "I could show you an experience you'll never forget."

It was a lie. He wouldn't remember a thing.

His eyes widened, and he swallowed hard, clearly captivated by my words. I could practically taste his desire.

"But... here?" He stammered, glancing around nervously. "Isn't there somewhere more... private?"

I chuckled softly, running a finger along his jawline. "Don't worry, darling. I know just the place."

I took his hand and led him towards the back exit of the bar. Juliet shuffled up behind us. I didn't need to hunt on Juliet's behalf—she was as skilled as any vampire. But in her current condition, I knew she wouldn't be on her A game. As hungry as she was, she might have ripped the man to shreds in the middle of the bar if I wasn't taking the lead.

When we got into the alley, I pushed the man against the brick. I could see the *desire* in his eyes. Cupids might stoke someone's lusts, but this was more than that. Vampires didn't enthrall their victims using sexual desire. We inspired *reverence.* Worship. With a snap of my fingers, if

I wished, he'd drop to his knees and lick the dirt from my boot.

Not that I wanted that. I mean, sure, my boots could use a good polishing. But saliva is nasty. Who wants someone's *spit* on their foot? The point is that when I had someone hooked, all their hard limits went out the door. The only thing on this poor sod's mind was me... more specifically, how he could *please* me.

The answer was simple. His *blood* was what I craved. It's what Juliet needed. And why would I take her out to eat if I wasn't going to get a bite as well?

When we were done, he'd pass out. He'd remember nothing at all thanks to his intoxicated condition. If he *thought* he remembered what happened, well, he'd tell no one. He'd have to explain why a man of his stature was at a hole-in-the-wall watering hole. Not to mention, if by some fluke he ever spoke of the encounter, who would believe him?

I held my hand over the man's mouth as I sank my fangs into his jugular. I didn't want his *moans* to elicit unnecessary attention. As his blood flooded my mouth, I motioned Juliet over. She bit his neck on the other side.

I don't know if my feelings for Juliet were returning, or if it was just my memory playing tricks on my body, but for a moment everything was as it should be. My free hand found Juliet's, our fingers interlacing, as we drank as much blood as our chosen victim could afford to lose.

When we were done, I lowered the man to the ground. Someone would find him, eventually. The enzymes in a vampire's saliva could heal a bite-wound in seconds. No one would know what really happened.

Juliet kissed me on the cheek. "Thanks, babe. That's what I needed."

I tilted my head. "Are you feeling something for me again?"

Juliet squeezed my hand. "I wish I did. But I'm acting 'as if.' What I feel right now is a blood rush."

I nodded. "Same. But what about your rage?"

Juliet narrowed her eyes. "I think I got it out of my system in hell. Or maybe being staked reset my system, somehow."

"I don't know. Wouldn't your feelings for me return, too? I wouldn't count on things being normal again. That cupid magic might find another way to affect you, eventually."

"Or it won't," Juliet sighed. "What if being staked also removed our connection, the blood bond? What if *that's* why I'm still not feeling what I did for you before?"

I frowned, deep in thought. What if she was right? What if the stake had severed the bond between us? The mere thought sent an echo through the void in my chest.

All that mattered for the time being was that we had enough focus to get the job done. We still had a mission to complete. We needed to kill a few cupids to free Mel, Muggs, and Alice.

Unless all we had to do was *stake* them... would that free them the way it might have released Juliet from the cupid's influence? We didn't know for sure that's what happened to Juliet. Until we knew more, we had to stick to the original plan. And I had to keep an eye on Juliet. It was *rage* that the cupid's magic stoked in her before. What would it be the next time if the magic infected a different part of her mind this time around?

Chapter 7

THE ALLEY WAS RANK with the copper tang of blood mixed with rotting garbage from a nearby dumpster. Sirens wailed in the distance. I hardly noticed. We were in a major city, after all.

"Think it's got something to do with the cupids?" Juliet asked, nudging the unconscious business executive with her steel-toed boot.

"Could be anything," I said. Though, given what the cupids were up to, I doubted the city's emergency personnel would have the manpower to prioritize petty criminals. From what we'd seen at the Ridley Hotel, the chaos that followed these cupids would demand an all-hands-on-deck response from the local authorities. "Then again, there's no telling how far this nonsense has spread."

Juliet's pink hair glowed under the soft hue of a nearby street lamp which cast a single swath of light into the alley. "We should check it out. Scope things, then rally the crew."

I hesitated. We needed the team for a proper hunt. But Mel usually had intelligence ready before we mobilized the Underground. She monitored police scanners, hacked local systems, whatever it took to get us the information we required. Without Mel's intel, we were flying blind. Perhaps some recon would do more good than harm.

"I don't know, Jinx. Just the two of us?"

Juliet smirked, hand on her hip. "We're two badass vampire bitches. Don't tell me you're scared."

"Hardly." I patted my leather pants, feeling the arrow tucked inside beside my wand. "I've still got one of their damned darts. But those winged freaks move fast. It took all of us to catch one that we had pinned down in my throne room. What shot do we have killing one of those bastards out in the open? And if we miss, we might lose our chance. I'd feel better if we had backup."

"So we'll call them. Hailey's got a phone, right?" Juliet's grin widened, exposing the tips of her fangs. "We'll check things out first. If it's serious, we ring the bell."

I wavered, staring down the alley as the sirens wailed. We'd just fed, so we had plenty of strength and speed to spare. We could examine the situation in a matter of minutes. What did we have to lose? Besides, if those sirens meant the cupids were on a tear, we had to know.

"Alright," I said finally. "But we *don't* engage until the team arrives unless we have no choice. We go stealth. In and out."

Juliet and I locked eyes, red meeting red, and nodded. In a blur of preternatural speed, we raced towards the sirens.

The flashing lights led us to the fire station. Four police cruisers were parked outside, sirens flashing silently.

"The cops were called to the fire station?" Jinx cocked an eyebrow. "That's... odd, to say the least."

I shrugged. "Crime can happen anywhere. It might be unusual, but that doesn't mean this is a cupid problem."

As we approached the fire station, I could already feel the tension building within me. Something was off. The air was heavy, as if tainted by a malevolent force. Juliet didn't feel it. She wasn't a witch. But as much as I hated to admit it, and hoped this wasn't a cupid issue, the signs were there.

Curious now, we crept inside. The sight that greeted us was one of total mayhem. Firefighters and cops were wrapped in passionate embraces, lost in each other's arms. Some were half-undressed already, urgent hands roving.

"Damn," Juliet tilted her head, spying a policeman and fireman already stripped down, one on all fours in front of the other. "I don't think *that's* what night sticks are for."

I shuddered. "Oh God. Sometimes I envy Muggs. I'm never going to get that image out of my head."

Juliet snickered. "Providence's finest *hard* at work!"

My lips twitched despite the gravity of the situation. "Whatever brought the cops here, there's definitely a cupid nearby."

Juliet tilted her head, listening. "There," she whispered, pointing towards the fire pole. Sure enough, I caught a glimpse of mangled wings fluttering playfully as the cupid slid down again and again, oblivious to us.

"That might be our guy," Juliet said. "The one who got Mel and the others. If we take him out now, we might fix this." Her muscles coiled, ready to spring.

I hesitated. "Maybe. But if we screw up, he'll bolt and we'll lose him." I pulled out my phone and shot a quick text to Hailey, updating her. "Let's wait for backup. We can try to contain this, but I don't want to risk letting him escape."

Juliet's face fell, but she nodded. "Yeah, you're right. We should play it safe."

I let out a breath, glad she would not fight me on this. Juliet had a habit of leaping before looking in situations like these.

My phone buzzed. Hailey and the others were on their way, but it would still be at least ten minutes. We needed to keep the cupid distracted and contained.

I scanned the room, taking in the writhing mass of bodies. "This hasn't turned violent yet, but once it does, well, those cops are all armed. It'll be a bloodbath."

Juliet grinned. "Sounds delicious."

I furrowed my brow. A demented sentiment—not uncommon among vampires. Still, we were well fed. Letting the situation devolve into a vampire buffet wasn't the agenda. "Look, the cops and I aren't exactly on the best of terms. But we can't let that happen. And it's just a matter of time before shit goes south if we can't maintain the situation until the team arrives."

"A cupid is a chaos creature," Juliet nodded. "We know it gets off on wreaking havoc. What if we can make a little chaos of our own? Maybe that will keep the cupid entertained enough to leave the situation as it is."

I nodded. "Once the cupid fires more arrows, we know what will happen. They'll start killing each other out of jealous passion. That's the cupid's end-game. How can we possibly slow it down?"

Juliet snickered. "Well, we already have half-dressed and undressed police officers and fighters. Add a white guy in a headdress, a construction worker, and a soundtrack..."

I rolled my eyes. "Good Lord."

"The NC-17 Village People!"

I held my clenched fists firm on my hips. *Don't laugh, Mercy. Once you start...*

"I will not dignify that comment with a response. This is *serious*. We need a legitimate distraction."

Juliet winked at me. "I've got this. If it works and you get a clean shot at the cupid, take it. No need to wait for the team."

"What are you planning?" I asked, but before I finished my question Juliet was halfway across the firehouse and pulling a hose from one of the trucks.

She was moving so fast that even with my trained eye, all I saw was a blur. She must've hooked up the hose somewhere because when she finally stopped, holding the hose with both hands, a powerful stream erupted towards the ceiling. The water sprayed and cascaded down like a torrential rainstorm. It soaked everyone in the room, dousing their passionate flames. Sounds of surprise and confusion filled the air as the chaos turned into utter chaos.

I shook my head, half-amused and half-impressed. That girl never ceased to amaze me. She certainly *aimed* to please.

As the water continued to rain down, the cupid fluttered its wings furiously, trying to avoid getting wet. It looked around, clearly agitated by the sudden change in the atmosphere. It hadn't expected this level of resistance.

But it didn't take long before the cupid fired back with a trademark strike. But Juliet intercepted the cupid's arrow with a forceful blast of water.

Then she turned the hose on the little bastard and sent him flying into the wall like a bug on a windshield.

The cupid shrieked what must've been a curse in Cupidish. Soaking wet, he flapped his wings to no avail.

Holy shit, I thought to myself. *Who would have thought that water, of all things, was the best weapon we had against these cupids?*

Taking advantage of its momentary disadvantage, I retrieved the cupid's arrow from my pocket, gripping it tightly in my hand. In mere seconds, standing over the cupid, I plunged the arrow right into the little shit's heart.

But nothing happened.

What the...

All I could think was that it wasn't just any cupid's arrow that would do the trick. A cupid had to be killed by *its own* arrow.

As if this situation wasn't difficult enough as it was.

All it took was that split-second pause. That *moment* of confusion. The next thing I knew, three more arrows struck me straight in the chest.

I grabbed one of them, intent on using it against my assailant. But the arrow was already used—it dematerialized in my grip.

"Damn it!" I screamed.

I tried to grab the cupid's quiver, but the wily fucker slipped away before I could snag it.

Thump. Tha-thump. Tha-thump.

My heartbeat? What the hell. Each successive beat closer together than the last.

A vampire's heart only beat a few times per minute, if that. Mine was racing like I was a couch potato on a treadmill.

I dropped to my knees. A tingle spread through my body, intensified on the fingertips of my left hand. A freaking heart attack? How in damnation was this possible?

Mercy... my love...

It wasn't Juliet's voice. It was another voice. A voice I knew too well. Was it real, or a figment of my imagination?

No, it wasn't Ladinas either. I'd be grateful if it was.

I blacked out. The heartbeat stopped. And when I opened my eyes, I saw him.

The dragon. Trapped in a void dimension. And somehow I was there with him.

He shifted into a human-like form, blond hair, green scaled armor.

"Oblivion." I clenched my fists. "I should have known."

"I am the father of chaos. The cupids are among my children. Did you really think you could trap me here without my kin coming to my aid?"

"How did you take me here? What the hell happened?"

Oblivion shrugged. "Your body remains where it was. You weren't staked. The cupids' magic comes from me. Since it was *my magic* that stopped your heart, it was only natural your spirit would come home *to me.*"

I shook my head. "This won't work. My friends will bring me back. Tell me how to stop these cupids or else."

Oblivion laughed. "Or else what? You'll throw me into another dimension? Oh, wait..."

"I'll kick your scaly ass. Somehow."

"Sure you will," Oblivion shook his head. "Or maybe I'll just hitch a ride back home with you. I am but a spirit, after all. And your spirit is here, ready to meld with mine like before. Already primed by my magic. All I have to do is get on the bus."

"I'll be damned before I let you back to earth." I clenched my fists. I was only a spirit in this dimension, but I felt as *real* and physical as ever.

Oblivion laughed. "Wouldn't be the first time I rode the Mercy bus, you know. How about a good fuck for old times' sake? What do you say?"

The chaos dragon wanted one thing. He was named for his deepest desire. All he wanted was to devolve the universe into its original state of chaos. He wanted to eliminate *existence* itself.

"Let me make one thing clear. I do *not* consent. And I won't let you out of this prison no matter what."

"You don't have a choice," Oblivion said as he wrapped his arms around me. "And your friends won't leave you here. They'll bring you back one way or another. All it'll take is a little magic and when you wake up, well..."

I struggled against Oblivion's grip. "Let go of me! I'm not taking you back with me!"

"There's no place like home, Mercy. No place like home..."

"Kiss my dead ass!"

Oblivion laughed. "Fear not. For I shall be with you always. Until the *end of the age...* and beyond."

Chapter 8

I AWOKE WITH A start, my eyes flying open to see Juliet, Hailey and Mel peering down at me. I was sprawled across the velvet couch in my underground throne room, the fabric now stained with dried... remnants of the cupid-induced orgy.

Disoriented, I blinked hard, trying to clear the fog from my mind. It took a moment before I realized—I was back. Back in the Underground, our sanctuary beneath the city.

"What happened?" I croaked, my throat dry. "Why is Mel out of her cell?"

"We handled it, Mercy," Juliet said, her voice steady and reassuring. Ever the loyal friend, her pink hair and piercings belying her inner strength. "Hailey killed the cupid. We got here just after you passed out."

I struggled to sit up, my limbs heavy and clumsy. Juliet gripped my arm, helping me upright.

"Lucky for me, that must have been the one that shot me," Mel chimed in. She avoided my gaze, clearly embarrassed. "One minute I was... well, you know. Making a damn fool of myself pining over you." She laughed nervously. "The next, I was thinking clearly again. Thank God."

My mind raced, trying to connect the disjointed pieces. If the cupid was dead, and Mel was back to normal...

"What about Muggs?" I asked urgently. "The same cupid shot him too. Why isn't he here?"

The three of them exchanged uneasy glances. No one had an answer.

Something was very wrong. We had to find Muggs before it was too late. But first, there was something I had to tell them. Something they would not like.

"When that cupid struck me, something happened," I began. My voice was steady, betraying none of the anxiety churning within. "My heart raced. Then it stopped. But I didn't end up in vampire hell. I was... somewhere else."

I took a deep breath. No turning back now.

"I was with Oblivion."

Juliet's eyes widened in alarm. "That's impossible! It must have been a nightmare or hallucination. There's no way-"

"It was real," I insisted, cutting her off. The words tumbled out in a rush. "I've been to hell before. It was just like that, except the location was, well, different."

Hailey sighed. "The cupid's magic, it's chaos magic, just like Oblivion uses."

I nodded. "I think when my heart stopped, it created some kind of link."

Horror dawned on Mel's face. "If that's true... we need to find Adam. Have him take us to the pocket dimension, see if Oblivion is still trapped there."

"No." My voice was sharp. As much as I wanted answers, we had more pressing concerns. "It's too dangerous right now. We need to focus on finding Muggs before something terrible happens."

I took a deep breath, bracing myself for what came next.

"And you need to lock me up. Just in case Oblivion really is inside me."

Juliet grabbed my hand, distraught. "Mercy, no! We need you. We'll find another way—"

"We don't have time to argue," I said gently. "You weren't there when Oblivion possessed me. If you were, you'd understand. We can't let him use me again."

"I won't let that happen!" Juliet insisted.

"No offense," Mel sighed. "If Oblivion gets a foothold with Mercy again, there won't be much you can do to stop it."

Hailey pressed her lips together. "And given your condition, how much that chaos magic has messed with you, we can't be totally sure you're back to normal. If there's any magic left in you from the cupid, it might not matter if the one that shot you is dead. Oblivion will be able to use it, to activate it again."

"Then lock me up with Mercy!"

Mel shook her head. "I was shot, too. We can't lock everyone up. And Mercy is right. We need to find out what happened to Muggs. We need to bring him home."

"And save Alice," I added. "She's potentially more dangerous than any of us. The cupid that shot her is still out there wreaking havoc. If Oblivion can use anyone who has been shot by a cupid, Alice will be the biggest threat we have to worry about. Myself excluded."

"And if Alice still thinks she's in love with Muggs because of the cupid," Mel added, "if we find Muggs, we'll find Alice."

"If he's not dead already," Pauli added. He hadn't said a word since I woke up, which was out of character. "What? I'm not trying to be a party pooper here. I love parties, and no one likes poop. That's why I take daily enemas! Keeps all my *parties* doodie free!"

I grunted. I didn't need to ask what kind of parties he was talking about. "What's your point, Pauli?"

"Keep your friends close. Keep your enemas closer! You know, in case your friends become something more!"

I grunted. "Not about that, dumbass! What's your point about Muggs?"

"All I'm saying—it's a possibility. Muggs might be dead already. Mercy, you said it yourself. If the cupid that enthralled him is dead, what's stopping him from coming home?"

"That's what I need all of you to find out! He might *not* be dead and needs our help. And we could certainly use his!"

"No one's disputing that," Juliet said. "But are you sure you're in any condition to go on a rescue mission?"

"Lock me up. I'll be fine. You're right. I can't be out there where Oblivion might use me if he's inside of me somehow, waiting for an opportunity. But we *need* Muggs. Because if Oblivion is inside of me, he's the only one who can send me away to another dimension."

"We're not locking you up," Juliet said firmly. "We need you out there with us."

I shook my head. "It's too dangerous. What if Oblivion takes control of me again?"

"We'll cross that bridge when we come to it," Juliet insisted. "Right now, finding Muggs is our top priority. If he's at all compromised, he'll need you, his sire, to get him straight. We can't do this without you, Mercy."

I hesitated. She was right, but so was I. Our chances of saving Muggs were greater if I was there. The risk of unleashing Oblivion was also higher if I exposed myself to more cupids. Then again, what was I going to do? Hide out forever? Oblivion was a void-dragon. The absence of existence—including the absence of time—was his specialty. If Oblivion needed an opportunity to manifest, my team could lock me away for centuries and he'd bide his time. All I knew was that the last time Oblivion took me over, I was vulnerable. I'd just found out that Ladinas and Alice had started a relationship in another dimension without me. I was heartbroken, and I let my rage get a foothold. That's what Oblivion exploited to manifest.

Right now, well, I wasn't angry. I was numb. But if all that magic in me found some emotion to exploit, something to use to open the door for Oblivion, we'd all be fucked.

"I'll come with you on one condition," I said, taking Juliet's hands in mind. "The second I feel him trying to take over, I want you to take me out. Stake me, send me to hell. Do whatever you need to do."

Juliet nodded solemnly. "I will. But it won't come to that."

I hoped she was right. I *hoped* all that happened after that cupid impaled me with its arrows really was a nightmare. But that was a dream. My gut told me that what had happened *was* real, and that Oblivion's threat wasn't hollow.

I also knew I had to face him. And I'd literally damn myself to hell before I let that scaly bastard use me again.

"Alright, let's move," I said, shoving my misgivings aside. "Muggs and Alice are still out there. We find them, we find the cupid controlling them. And we end that winged bastard once and for all."

"No," Juliet added. "We end *all* those winged bastards. And we foil Oblivion's plan to come back before he gets a chance."

Chapter 9

I FELT LIKE SOMEONE had dropped an anvil on my chest. I was usually cool under pressure. I'd seen enough evil shit in my time that you'd think nothing would get to me. Not to mention, with my emotions turned off, it was strange that I was so uneasy. It was almost like my body was responding as if I was anxious—because with the thought that Oblivion might be lying low inside of me waiting for a chance to spring out and use me again was downright terrifying.

What that dragon did to me before...

I shuddered at the thought of it happening *again*. The last time I was under Oblivion's influence, I nearly destroyed the world. I had plans and everything. I was going to do it. He had me so damn drunk on his lies that I was convinced he was going to make me a goddess.

But to Oblivion, I was a means to an end. And he wasn't the kind of villain who didn't learn his lessons. He wouldn't let us trap him the same way we did the last time.

"Got anything on Alice and Muggs' location?" I asked Mel. Her fingers flew across the tablet as she scanned Providence PD reports.

"Even after all this time, most of the activity remains centered on the Ridley Hotel," she said. "Multiple units are still responding to calls there."

Juliet frowned, brow furrowing. "Doesn't make sense. We ran into those crazed cupids just outside of headquarters. That's miles away from the hotel. What's so damn special about that hotel that the focus remains there?"

I met her gaze and gave a grim nod. She had a point.

"Perhaps there's a convergence around there," Hailey suggested. "These cupids are otherworldly. They had to come from somewhere. Isn't Willie still guarding the convergence near Exeter?"

I nodded. "If anything came through there, we'd know about it."

"Which means there has to be another gateway somewhere that the cupids used to get here," Hailey said. "But I doubt these creatures came here of their own accord. Someone summoned them."

I shook my head. "They're chaos creatures. Loyal to Oblivion."

Hailey pinched her chin. "If you *really* saw Oblivion when that cupid thrust its arrows into your heart, perhaps that was the plan all along. But there must be someone out there doing Oblivion's bidding to cause all this to begin with. A lot of random shit can come out of a convergence, but those portals to other dimensions and worlds don't form bridges to whoever wants to use them. There are only a handful of beings across all the universes who can manipulate a convergence."

"Makes sense." I took a deep breath and held it a moment before I let it out. "But we can worry about who started this shit later. First, we have to stop the cupids, and if Oblivion manifests in me…"

"I know," Juliet said with a sigh. "We still have to stop him *if* he shows up."

"You may have to stop *me,* Juliet. You promised. If it comes to it, I'm trusting you'll do what has to be done. Shouldn't be hard, since we feel *nothing* for each other anymore."

An awkward silence filled the air. I knew it was bullshit when I said it. It also came out harsher than I intended it. But why would she care? She was as numb as I was.

Yeah, Juliet and I weren't swooning over one another anymore, but things were more complicated than that. We both knew we were happy when we were together. We enjoyed each other's company. That meant something. But if she *had* to stake me, well, being numb to one another would make it easier than it would have been before all this happened.

"Sorry. I didn't mean it like that."

Juliet rested a hand on her knee. "I get it. But you're right. This condition might make it easier to do what has to be done, but it's no blessing in disguise. It won't be easy, regardless."

"You gave me your word." I focused forward, unable to make myself look her in the eye.

"I did." Her voice was cold. Music to my ears—because the only tune I could tolerate at the moment was a dirge. It was what the situation required.

I took a deep breath and turned to face the team. "Enough talk. Time for action. Everyone arm up. We're moving out in ten."

I led the way to the armory, my duster billowing behind me. As I stepped through the doorway, the lights flickered on automatically. The armory was stocked with enough weapons and ammo to arm a small militia.

Juliet went straight for the crossbows. The compact recurve bows were easy to maneuver in close quarters, and the bolts could be fitted with stakes, explosives or grappling hooks. I chose a set of stainless steel bolts tipped with oak. "Don't hesitate. If we have to take out Alice, that's what we'll have to do. Anything to help Muggs."

"Presuming another cupid has not shot him since then," Juliet added. "We don't know what's happened since we left them around the hotel."

"Good point," I nodded as I picked up an extra magazine of wood-tipped bullets and my trusty Glock.

Juliet tested the tension on her crossbow before slinging it over her shoulder. She grabbed a bandolier of bolts and a pair of silver daggers to strap to her thighs. I tried not to stare as she strapped the blades on, but I couldn't help admiring her warrior physique.

Mel opted for a 9mm pistol and filled her pockets with extra magazines. Hailey just shook her head when I offered her a weapon.

"I don't use weapons," she said. "I might be the world's most proficient blood witch. I couldn't hit a target with a gun from ten feet away. I'll stick to what I know."

I nodded. "You and Pauli should focus on any cupids we encounter. Remember, if we can eliminate the cupids, everything else will resolve itself. But I can't count on that. I'm going to focus on rescuing Muggs."

Pauli tilted his head. "Honey, Pauli is used to handling more than one... thing... at a time. I'll help Hailey with the cupids, but if I get a chance, I can zap in and out of wherever Muggs might be and get him back to you in seconds."

I nodded at Pauli. "Good thinking. Your abilities could come in handy if we need to extract Muggs quickly."

We loaded into the SUVs and sped toward the Ridley Hotel. Mel drove while Juliet and I took the backseat. The mood was tense. We didn't know exactly what we'd encounter at that hotel, but it was bound to be a shitshow.

After a few minutes of silence, Mel glanced at us in the rearview mirror. "So...you two have any feelings coming back yet?"

I sighed, staring out the window into the night. "No. I'm still numb. The magic did a number on me."

Juliet shook her head, fiddling with a bolt for her crossbow. "Same here. I wish I could feel something again, but it's just empty inside."

Mel laughed, turning her eyes back to the road. I furrowed my brow. "What's so funny?"

"Because that's the nature of relationships," Mel said. "Cupid's arrow or not, blood bonds or whatever, infatuation fades with *every* relationship. You can't sustain those dizzy, head-over-heels feelings forever. At some point, you have to make a decision—do you commit to truly loving that person? When you do, love stops being an emotion and becomes a choice."

I pondered her words. She was right. If people only stayed together on cloud nine, no one's relationship would last beyond a year or two. Happiness doesn't have to be contingent on a feeling. Perhaps Juliet and I had been given a gift—a chance to build something real now that the artificial passion had worn off. I mean, if we were human, it would be more obvious. Juliet and I were beautiful despite approaching the second half of our second century of existence. Humans age, get wrinkly, their youthful beauty fades. At some point, marriages that last have to move beyond physical attraction. Human eyes have to adapt to see a beauty that's more than skin-deep.

For once, I realized humans had an advantage in that regard. Just because vampires kept their beauty didn't mean that our relationships could endure based on it. Relationships caught up in the physical never grow. At some point, love has to mature. If it doesn't, it won't be half as satisfying as it could be.

Maybe that's why so many vampires struggle with their relationships. We think that our ability to live indefinitely gives us an advantage. We can be *together forever...*

But very few vampires stay together for longer than a few years, a decade at most.

I reached over and took Juliet's hand. She looked at me and smiled. There was still a connection, buried beneath the magic's residue. We would find it again. Or we wouldn't. Because our connection *before* would not last, anyway.

I squeezed Juliet's hand, feeling a small spark of something stir within me. It wasn't the raging fire, but a gentle warmth. Not an emotion, but knowledge that if we wanted to make things work, if we really enjoyed each other, then no cupid could spoil it. And all we needed was a spark—something to nurture into a steady blaze.

"When did you get so wise about relationships?" I asked Mel, a wry smile touching my lips.

She shrugged, eyes on the road ahead. "I watch Dr. Phil. I know things."

Juliet and I both laughed at that. Leave it to Mel to gain romantic insights from daytime TV. But she wasn't wrong. What Juliet and I had went deeper than manufactured passion. It would take time and care, but we could rebuild what we'd lost. It wouldn't be the same as it was—but it *could be* something better. If we made the choice to pursue it.

If that damn dragon didn't take me over again...

I caught Mel's eye in the rear view mirror. She winked at me, then focused back on driving. We were getting close to the hotel now. People were doing it like dogs in the street all around us. Quite a sight. It dawned on me that even after we killed the cupids, these people would come to their senses totally confused about the whole affair. And *affairs* will have been had. The chaos wouldn't end. How many marriages and families might be *screwed over* by this bullshit?

The cupids stoked passion. The rage that followed was *human*. Passions running roughshod over everything else. Every emotion had its place, but everything had to be kept in balance and perspective. When one thing, like lust, rules the roost, everything else goes askew. Passion stokes envy. Envy becomes rage, and rage turns violent. But that wasn't the end. When this was over, there'd be shame, guilt, and regret.

Killing the cupids might cut off the root of the problem—but it was only the beginning of the chaos that Oblivion and his winged minions craved.

Mel's advice helped me when it came to my relationship with Juliet. If we wanted it, we could make this work even if our feelings never returned. But that simple insight also highlighted the gravity of the problem the cupids caused.

Lives were already altered. Relationships were probably destroyed. In the past, all I ever thought about was killing the bad guys. But now, I saw things differently. Maybe it was because I'd had a relationship that was affected by all this bullshit. Maybe I'd just grown up a little. I never thought about the long term impact that my enemies had on human lives—but even if my team and I succeeded, if we won the battle, the echoes of Oblivion's chaos would resonate for years... for entire lifetimes.

Chapter 10

The Ridley Hotel loomed before us, pulsing neon and pounding bass leaking from its façade. Our SUVs skidded to a stop amidst the abandoned cop cars, their lights still flashing blue and red across the empty street.

But the streets were empty. No cupids flying through the air. No infected humans banging one out on the sidewalks. Aside from the awful beats coming from inside the hotel, the place was eerily quiet.

I stepped out of the SUV, the din of shitty techno music assaulting my ears. My team emerged behind me—Jinx, her pink hair glowing in the street lights; Mel, face set in a mask of determination; Hailey, practically vibrating with excitement, always eager for a fight; and Pauli, shaking his skinny ass to the beat as he shimmied out of the vehicle.

Antoine and his vamps clustered close, awaiting instruction. I met Antoine's gaze. "Guard the exit. No cupids get away, got it? And if you see Alice, restrain her. Do whatever you need to do. Don't let her slip away."

He nodded, though I saw cynicism in his eyes. Restraining Alice would prove a challenge, but they were armed with crossbows and wood-tipped bullets good for the job. "You have my word."

I turned back to my team. Jinx and Mel watched me steadily, prepared for anything. Hailey bounced on her toes, already amped for the fight ahead.

"Remember our tentative plan," I said. "Hailey focuses on the cupids. Pauli helps wherever he's needed. The rest of us grab Muggs and deal with Alice."

"Tentative plan," Mel added. "Because there's no telling what we're about to encounter inside."

"Exactly," I confirmed with a nod. "We have to be ready to adjust our attack on the fly. But we've all faced worse. We can do this."

"Let's do this," Jinx growled, cracking her knuckles.

I bared my fangs in a vicious grin. "Happy Valentine's Day, everyone."

We were armed and ready. Whatever we were going to face, well, the only thing I knew for sure was that *chaos* was the word of the day. And we were about to instill some much-needed order.

Saving Muggs was the primary objective. Killing cupids was secondary, but if we could end all of this at once, why not take the opportunity?

We stalked through the front doors, the pounding music swelling to surround us.

The lobby was empty, but the scent of sweat, sex, and blood hung heavy in the air. My fangs throbbed as I followed the scent deeper into the hotel.

The ballroom doors were wide open. I didn't hesitate, just strode right in with my team at my back.

What I saw made me pause for only a second.

Alice sat on a throne on the dais at the front of the room, wearing nothing but a smug smile. Dozens of naked men were prostrated at her feet, moaning and writhing. One was enthusiastically licking her toes, his ass wiggling in the air.

Disgust rose in my throat like bile. This was not the Alice I knew. The cupids had turned her into some parody of herself, more like a succubus than a vampire, reveling in her own corruption.

I stalked forward, my boots thumping a counterpoint to the pounding music. "Alice," I snarled. "Snap out of it."

She tilted her head, looking me over with a slow, considering gaze. Then she laughed, the sound throbbing with dark promise.

"Make me."

I clenched my fists, rage burning through my veins.

But I couldn't give in to anger. Not now. I couldn't give Oblivion a foothold. I took a deep breath and approached the dais, meeting her glowing pink gaze. The cupid magic was pouring off her in waves, visibly rippling the air around her.

"You're not yourself," I said, forcing my voice to stay calm. I knew she wouldn't listen to reason—cupid magic isn't rational. But I had to try—more for my sake than hers. "The cupids are manipulating you. Fight it, Alice."

"Worship me," she purred, leaning forward to display her pale breasts. The surrounding men moaned in unison, surging toward her like starving dogs. She waved them back with a negligent hand.

She wasn't the one possessed by Oblivion, but I knew what his magic felt like. He'd once convinced me I was destined to be divine. Even without his direct influence, his power had tempted Alice the same.

"I won't ask again." I folded my arms over my chest, well aware of the others flanking me. Juliet's cool, restraining presence anchored me, while Hailey bristled, ready to unleash a spell at a moment's notice. We were all on edge.

Alice tilted her head again, eyes narrowing. For a moment, I thought I saw a flicker of recognition in their depths. But it was gone in an instant, replaced by cruel amusement.

"I'm not asking at all." She waved the cupids forward. "Bow down and kiss my feet. You might be a queen, but I'm your goddess!"

They descended from the rafters in a flurry of pink and white, a dozen of the little bastards, arrows notched and aimed at our hearts. My team tensed, ready to fight, but again Alice raised her hand.

"Hold," she purred, and the cupids obeyed, hovering in place.

Dread coiled in my gut. Why weren't the cupids attacking?

Because this was a trap. Because Oblivion was using Alice as bait to get to me. I didn't have any reason to believe that Oblivion was communicating with Alice, but his cupid minions were. And they had one goal—to bring their master back.

I swallowed hard, trying to stay calm. So long as I could keep my shit together, Oblivion was *my* prisoner. He was bound to me and couldn't do shit.

"Where's Muggs?" I demanded, ignoring the cupids for now. If they wanted to attack, they would have already done so. This was a game for them. For Alice *and* Oblivion.

Alice's lips curled into a cruel smirk. "Oh, he didn't want to play nice. I had to put him in time-out."

Fury was begging to boil up inside me, hot and acrid. If she'd hurt Muggs—but I couldn't lose control. Not now. I gritted my teeth, fists clenching at my sides. "What did you do to him?"

"Wouldn't you like to know?" Her eyes gleamed with malicious glee. "Maybe I staked him. Maybe I ripped out his heart. Or maybe--"

"Enough!" Hailey snapped, taking a step forward. Pink light glowed around her hands, the air crackling with power. The cupids tensed, arrows twitching in her direction, but Alice held up a hand.

"Not yet," she purred. "I'm having too much fun."

Hailey's eyes narrowed, but she didn't attack. Not yet. We couldn't risk it, not with Muggs' life on the line and a dozen cupids ready to turn us into pincushions.

I took a deep breath and let it out slowly. Stay calm. Stay focused. Muggs was alive—he was my progeny, I could feel it. If she'd burned out his heart, I'd know. But that didn't mean he wasn't staked. Whatever the case, Alice was toying with us, trying to provoke me.

Well, she'd have to try harder than that. I put on a blank expression and examined my nails.

"Are we done posturing yet?" I asked. "Only some of us have lives to get back to. Places to go, people to save. You know how it is."

Alice's eyes flashed with rage, the cupids twitching in response. But she recovered quickly, forcing a laugh.

"You always had a smart mouth," she said. "It's why we got on so well—and why we fought so much." Her gaze softened, just for a moment, and again I thought I saw a flicker of the real Alice behind those glowing pink eyes.

"You're still in there," I said softly. "Fight him, Alice. Don't let Oblivion win."

"Oh, but he already has." Her smile turned vicious. "And now it's your turn."

She waved a hand, and the cupids surged forward, arrows at the ready. But before they could fire, Mel lunged in front of me, throwing up a magical shield. The arrows bounced off harmlessly, clattering to the floor.

"Nice try," Hailey said. She glanced at me, eyes hard. "We will not make this easy for you."

"How sweet," Alice purred. "The children have come to protect their mother. How utterly... predictable."

I gritted my teeth against the taunt, knowing she was trying to provoke me into attacking. But no matter how angry I got, I couldn't hurt Alice. Not really. Ladinas would never forgive me if I let her go villain in his absence. She'd been my enemy, and for a brief couple of years, she was my friend. I needed to save her. Even if it meant staking her temporarily. To do that, I had to stay calm.

"Call off your lap dogs," I said, "or I'll—"

"You'll what?" Alice leaned forward. "Go on. Threaten me. It's what you're good at, isn't it, Mercy? All bark and no bite."

"I don't want to hurt you," I said softly. "But I will if I must. Call them off."

"Or what?" Her eyes glowed brighter. "You can't stop me. You never could, and you never will. I am eternal, I am infinite, I am—"

"Oh, stuff it." I rolled my eyes. "You're being overdramatic. It's annoying."

Alice hissed, the sound echoing through the ballroom. The cupids buzzed in agitation, their arrows nocked and ready to fire. The humans under Alice's thrall tensed, hands curling into claws.

"You dare mock me?" Alice said, her voice deathly quiet. "After everything I've done for you, after every sacrifice, you stand there and mock me?"

"I'm not mocking you," I said. "I'm telling you the truth. Now call off your minions before this gets ugly."

"Or what?" Alice stood, the movement fluid and predatory. Her eyes glowed like twin suns. The cupid magic poured off her in waves, filling the room with pink light. "What will you do, Mercy? You're outnumbered. I am a goddess now, and you are merely an ant I can crush beneath my heel."

"Yeah, yeah." I waved a hand dismissively. She wasn't any stronger than she usually was. The only reason she had any power at all was because the cupids made a hundred or more humans *think* they were in love with her. And for some reason, she'd convinced them to serve her rather than kill one another to compete for her affection. "You're super scary. I get it. Now call them off."

Alice laughed, the sound reverberating through the ballroom, mocking me. "You don't get it, Mercy. You never will. I am no longer just Alice. I am the embodiment of the darkness that consumes all those who dare to defy Oblivion. You cannot defeat me because he's inside of you. He will fight with me to beat you."

The sound of Oblivion's laughter echoed in my mind. *I can help you, Mercy. Alice is just a tool. You are the one I truly desire. Let me out. I can take over the magic that's enthralled her. I can free your progeny. I can end this...*

I narrowed my eyes, ignoring Oblivion's honeyed words. He might promise me anything, but I knew the truth—he only wanted destruction. Yeah, he could end this. But he really wanted to end *everything*. He wanted to destroy *existence* itself.

"You can't control me anymore," I said firmly. "Last time I was heartbroken. I was vulnerable. This time, I've made my choice. And passion has nothing to do with it. I want to be with Juliet."

Oblivion just laughed, the sound grating in my mind. *You can resist me, little vampire, but you cannot defeat me.*

"If I don't give you a foothold, an emotion to exploit, you can't do shit," I shot back. I wasn't some lovesick fool like Alice. I had something real with Juliet. And if it wasn't for the cupids silencing my blood bond, I wouldn't have realized it. He'd done his worst. He'd expected he could manipulate us again by toying with our passions. But I wasn't the same heartbroken and pissed off girl I was when he took advantage of me before.

"You and me, Alice." I took two steps forward. "You spent more than a century trying to hunt me down with the Order of the Morning Dawn. I've wished you were dead more times than I can count. Recent alliances aside, what do you say we end this once and for all?"

Alice sneered at me. "About time. You and me. Keep your lackeys out of it and I'll do the same."

I smirked and gestured to Juliet, Hailey, Mel, and the rest. "Stay back. I'll finish this alone." They nodded back at me. This was the best chance we had to beat Alice and the cupids without unnecessary bloodshed. I turned back to Alice. "May the baddest bitch win."

I leapt at Alice, not holding anything back. She was ready for me, meeting my attack with supernatural speed and strength. We crashed together, exchanging blows that would have killed a human instantly. She was stronger than I expected. Something about the cupid magic inside of her gave her extra vigor.

As we fought, I could see the flicker of emotion in Alice's eyes. For a moment, she seemed conflicted. But then her expression hardened and she attacked again. She was determined to prove herself, to defeat me and win the favor of Oblivion.

Or at least beat me into a moment of weakness, to give Oblivion a chance to take me over. If she could stoke my anger, my resentment, anything...

But I was determined too. I wouldn't let her win, not when so much was at stake. I fought with everything I had, using every trick and technique I knew. But Alice was a skilled hunter, trained by the Order of the Morning Dawn to take down supernatural beings like me.

And I'd underestimated how much harder it was to fight without the aid of one's emotions. I could be cold, calculated, and strategic. But a little rage and fury can be fuel for the fire when in a fight. And Alice was boiling over with it.

Little by little, she gained the upper hand, pressing me back against a wall and pinning me there with her immense strength. But even in this position, I refused to give up.

"You can't beat me," Alice sneered, her fangs bared as she leaned in closer.

I gritted my teeth and pushed against her with all my strength, using my vampire speed to slip out from under her grasp. We continued our fight, both of us evenly matched in skill and power.

Then Alice seized an opening and landed a punch that sent me reeling.

"Mercy!" Juliet cried. I heard her footsteps moving toward me, but before she could intervene, Alice grabbed me and pulled me into a kiss.

What the hell? Why would she...

Power flooded out of me in a rush, and I heard Oblivion's laughter echoing in my mind. I had my answer. This wasn't about stoking my passion, making me vulnerable to Oblivion. Alice's plan was to *claim* Oblivion all along, to become his vessel.

But this wasn't all about what Alice wanted. She wasn't that stupid. She wasn't so foolish—not usually. It resulted from the cupid magic that warped her mind.

Alice stepped back, a triumphant grin on her face. But as I watched, her features changed. Her skin darkened to a scaly green, her eyes glowing bright pink. Fangs and claws lengthened, and she grew several inches taller.

Oblivion had taken her over.

The demon surveyed his new form appreciatively. "This will do nicely," he purred in Alice's voice.

He turned his gaze on me, eyes glowing with malevolent glee. I struggled to stand, my limbs trembling. Oblivion stalked closer, lifting me up by the throat and slamming me against the wall.

"You thought you could defeat me," he said with a mocking laugh. "You foolish girl. Did you really think you could hold me back forever? All I needed was a willing vessel."

He tossed me aside like a rag doll. I crashed to the floor, my vision swimming. Through the haze, I saw Juliet rush forward to attack Oblivion. But he swatted her away just as easily, sending her tumbling across the room.

"Now, I will finish what I started," Oblivion said, snapping the leg off a table, the broken end sharp. He strode over to me, raising the makeshift stake above his head. "Any last words?"

I gritted my teeth, summoning the last of my strength. "Go to hell."

Oblivion just laughed. "I was born there."

He thrust the stake down toward my chest. But at the last second, a flash of red light engulfed us. The stake stopped just short of piercing my heart.

I craned my neck to see Hailey behind us, chanting fiercely as she wove a spell. A shimmering blood-red barrier now surrounded Oblivion, holding him in place.

"This won't contain me for long," Oblivion growled. "You can only delay the inevitable. You cannot stop me."

Hailey hurried over and helped me to my feet. "We have to get out of here," she urged. "We're no match for him like this."

I hesitated, glancing at the barrier holding Oblivion at bay. We couldn't leave yet. Not without—

A familiar rainbow-patterned snake slithered into view, a lifeless body gripped in his coils. My heart sank as I recognized Muggs.

But Pauli deposited Muggs' body at my feet, then shifted back to his human form. "I found him staked in a closet," he explained. "But his heart is still intact in his chest. We can bring him back."

Relief flooded over me, followed by determination. We had what we came for. Now it was time to leave, regroup, and plan our next move.

I nodded to Hailey and Pauli. "Let's go."

We rushed out of the hotel, piling into our vehicles as the barrier around Oblivion finally shattered. The demon emerged in a blast of power, roaring with rage.

But we were already speeding off into the night, bruised and battered but ready to fight another day. Oblivion may have won this round, but the war wasn't over yet.

Chapter 11

I swept through the throne room, Muggs' limp body cradled in my arms. Gently resting him on the couch, I pulled out the stake embedded in his heart.

Muggs jolted awake with a gasp. "Back, ye devil dogs!" he cried. "Me arse is not fer business!"

Despite everything, I chuckled. His old-world accent and lingo shone through when he was under duress. "Welcome back to the land of the unliving, Muggs."

He blinked, regaining his bearings. "Mercy? What in blazes happened?"

"Well, you were staked. Obviously." I studied Muggs closely, ensuring no lasting damage had been done. "How are you feeling?"

Muggs patted himself down. "Aye, I'm right as rain. A little hungry. Thank the gods you brought me back when ye did."

I shook my head. "Don't thank me. Thank Pauli." I gestured to where Pauli stood, giving a small wave. "He's the one who found you and brought you back."

Muggs peered at Pauli, piecing it together. "Ah, so you're the colorful lad I've heard about! You have my gratitude." He smiled warmly.

Pauli grinned. "Anytime, honey."

I took a deep breath, bracing to break the news. "Muggs, I need to tell you what happened while you were out. I got hit by a whole quiver of cupid arrows. Sent my spirit straight to Oblivion."

Muggs grunted and rubbed his brow. If he had a headache, well, that was to be expected after returning from vampire hell. He was lucky that was all he was dealing with. If it was... there was no telling how bad things got. From the sound of it, I'd pulled him out of there just in time to spare him from becoming a hellhound's bitch.

"Oblivion hitched a ride back on my essence. To cut a bloody long story short, he skipped out of me and is now shacking up inside Alice."

I paused, letting the severity sink in. Muggs stared, stricken. "Alice. She staked me, didn't she? One minute I thought we were in love, the next..."

I nodded. "We killed the cupid that shot you. But not the one that got her. She realized what happened and thought to stop you before you could get in her way."

"But the situation is even graver now," I continued. "Oblivion is free in the mortal realm. And he aims to unmake the world, sending everything that exists into the void."

Muggs swallowed hard. "Gods above."

Muggs' countenance fell as the weight of my words settled on his shoulders.

"We have to stop him," Mel said, stepping forward. "If we get Adam here too, the two of you together can banish Oblivion back to the pocket dimension."

Muggs slowly shook his head. "That won't work. Not permanently. As long as those blasted cupids are free, Oblivion will always find a way back."

Juliet chimed in. "If we try to imprison Oblivion again, we'd just trap Alice right along with him." She crossed her arms. "And I mean, the downside there is…"

I rolled my eyes. "Yeah, yeah, I made a promise to Ladinas to protect her. But he's not here now, is he?"

My flippant tone masked the sinking feeling in my gut. Ladinas was gone, sentenced to a century trapped in the djinn's lamp. And I'd failed him—failed to keep Alice safe from Oblivion's corruption.

Juliet crossed the room to stand beside me, placing a hand on my shoulder. "Ladinas trusted you to protect Alice until his sentence in the lamp was over. But maybe…" She paused, brow furrowing. "Maybe seeing him again is the answer. If anyone can help Alice fight back against Oblivion's control, it's Ladinas."

I blinked, realization dawning. It was because of my relationship with Juliet that I'd prevented Oblivion from taking me over before. Admitting that Ladinas and Alice *belonged* together was a gigantic step for me. Especially how their relationship came about in the wake of my heartbreak. "You're right. She needs him if she's going to have any chance of prevailing here."

Juliet nodded. "His influence could be the key. If he can give Alice a spark of hope, enough to take control for just a split-second..."

I tilted my head. "What are you thinking? How will this destroy Oblivion?"

"If we trap Oblivion in the lamp with Ladinas..." Juliet continued, trailing off in thought. "Ladinas is basically a god in there. He could do whatever he wants to put Oblivion in his place."

I shook my head, grasping Juliet's arm. "That won't work. Not permanently. In a century, the original djinn returns, Ladinas leaves, and Oblivion goes free again. All we'd accomplish is kicking the damn can-o'-apocalypse down the road."

I met Juliet's gaze, my voice hardening. "But if we do this right... if Alice can fight off Oblivion herself, we might just have a shot at banishing him for good."

Juliet's eyes widened. "You mean, if Alice takes control..."

"She could use his own magic against him," I finished. "We can get rid of Oblivion and those blasted cupids in one fell swoop. Send them all to the pocket dimension without losing Alice."

Juliet bit her lip. "There's one more thing we have to consider."

I nodded, having already considered the risk. "Waking Ladinas from the lamp could be dangerous. He's only been in there a few months. His powers will still be weak, leaving him vulnerable."

Juliet met my gaze. "And we could hand Oblivion the weapon he needs to accomplish his goal. When a lamp is destroyed..."

"It creates a void portal, a doorway to suck the world out of existence..."

Juliet nodded. "But if Oblivion has his way, he'll unmake the world eventually, anyway. Using the djinn's lamp is a risk, but it's a risk with a reward. So long as we do nothing, we're all damned."

I let out a weary sigh, the weight of our predicament settling heavily on my shoulders. The djinn's lamp was hidden in a pocket dimension. Retrieving it was possible, but also risky. Mostly because we'd shattered the lamp in the pocket dimension. The entire place was basically a giant black hole. The lamp would have reconstituted itself, the only thing that remains in a realm that's basically as empty as the void, but we knew we'd have to recover it someday.

I just didn't expect we'd be going after the lamp so soon. I thought we still had a hundred years, minus a couple months, to figure out how we were going to pull that off.

And that was the least of our problems. All of this hinged on whether seeing Ladinas again would really give Alice the strength she needed to fight off Oblivion.

As much as it pained me to admit, Ladinas was never truly mine. He and Alice had a bond that transcended our complicated past. I had to believe their love was real. That it was enough to give Alice the strength she needed to fight off Oblivion's darkness.

"So this is how it ends," I said softly. "No matter what I used to feel for Ladinas, he and Alice are meant to be. I have to put my faith in that bond if we're going to get through this."

Juliet placed a gentle hand on my arm. "It's the only way, Mercy. You know that."

I nodded, hardening my resolve. "Then it's decided. We find the lamp, wake Ladinas, and pray Alice can harness his magic to kick Oblivion's ass back to the void where he belongs."

My voice took on a razor's edge. "That puffed up lizard has had his fun. Now it's time to show him what happens when he messes with my friends."

I turned to Muggs, my expression grim. "All this depends on you getting us into the pocket dimension Adam created, where he sent the lamp."

Muggs nodded, though his usual impish grin seemed strained. "Damn it. I forgot that Adam, Ramon, and Clarissa were out of town."

I sighed. After the ordeal with the djinn, I thought the young family needed a little time away from the chaos. So, Adam found a paradisiac dimension, a place they could spend quality time together without worrying about the next otherworldly threat. They brought a few humans along—a regular stable of virile men and women—all willing to open their veins for Clarissa's sake in exchange for a free vacation.

We could have used Adam's help. He was the heir to the Unseelie throne. Part-faerie, part-vampire, part-human. A unique combination that made him more powerful than pretty much any being I'd ever encountered—but he was also young, naïve, and deserved a chance to grow up without all the shit he was bound to encounter if he stayed with us in Exeter. What was the worst that could happen if they took off for a few months?

Little did I realize...

No matter. We didn't know how to locate them. That meant we had to rely on Muggs' teleportation abilities to get us into the dimension where Adam sent the lamp.

"Can you take us there to retrieve the lamp?" I asked.

Muggs grunted. "Yeah. I suppose I can. Adam showed me how to access that realm. It won't be a walk in the park. We don't know what kind of chaos we'll find there. How do you locate *something* in an abyss?"

I pinched my chin. "Well, if it's the only thing that exists in that dimension, it should stick out like a sore thumb."

Muggs shrugged. "Or we'll have to wade through an eternity of nothingness before we find it. When you're dealing with non-existence, the rules of space and time don't really apply. The point is, we don't have a clue what we'll discover when we go there. We might never find it."

"Or worse," Mel added. "Time might pass differently there than it does here. What if you go there, find the lamp, and return to find a year or more has passed and Oblivion and Alice already destroyed the world?"

"Not an issue." Muggs waved his bony hand through the air. "When Adam formed the pocket dimension, I knew Ladinas had to spend a hundred years in the lamp and that the original djinn wouldn't come looking for it until the same amount of time passed in this world. I instructed Adam to make sure the other dimension was as similar to this world as possible. To keep the time synced between both worlds, he placed that dimension as close to our fabric of reality as he could without putting our realm at risk."

"Brilliant!" I exclaimed. It was nice to have one potential complication ironed out in advance. Thank the gods for

Muggs' foresight in that regard. I knew there was a reason, or twelve, why I kept the old bloodsucking bastard around. "Let's get you a quick bite, Muggs. You'll need it after your trip to vampire hell. Then we'll head out. Everyone else—stand guard. If we don't come back, saving the world falls to you."

"I'm coming with you," Juliet added with a resolute nod. "Where you go, I go."

I grinned slightly. "Alright. Then, Hailey? You have things handled earth-side?"

Hailey chuckled. "You're putting me in charge?"

"Damn straight," I grinned. "You're the most powerful vampire-witch here. And you have *almost* as much world-saving experience as I do."

"Be careful," Mel added. "No pressure or anything. But the entire world depends on your success."

I snickered. "Right. No pressure. I swear, if humanity knew how many times I put my ass on the line for them, they'd throw me a freaking parade."

Juliet took my hand in hers. "If the world knew all the shit either of us had done in the past, they'd just as soon burn out our hearts."

I chuckled. "Yeah, that's true, too. But whatever. At least this time, we're saving the goddamn world or we'll die trying—together."

Chapter 12

The blood lingered on Muggs' lips like a guilty pleasure as we strode down the stone corridor. He swiped at it with his sleeve, licking the last drops from the corner of his mouth.

"Better?" I asked.

"Much," he rasped, a glint returning to his blind eyes. "I'll have the strength to rip us a portal, no problem."

We found Jinx in the armory, loading up on blades and bullets like we were gearing up for war. I almost laughed.

"You really think we'll need all that firepower in the void?"

Jinx shrugged, sliding a magazine into her Glock. "Doesn't hurt to be prepared."

I leaned against the wall, arms folded. "It's an empty dimension, Juliet. We're more likely to encounter a whole lot of nothing than anything worth shooting."

"Rather have it and not need it," she said, strapping a silver dagger to her thigh, "than need it and not have it."

Classic Jinx. She'd walk barefoot over hot coals for me, and I knew if trouble found us, she'd throw herself in its path without hesitation. But I hoped this would be a quick, uneventful trip. We had bigger problems back home if we didn't find Ladinas soon.

Jinx loaded the last shotgun shell and racked the pump. "I'm ready when you are."

I sighed. "Let's get this over with."

Muggs gathered us together in the center of the armory, gripping his oaken staff with both hands. He spun it overhead, chanting words in a language no one else knew. A whirling portal tore open the fabric of reality at the center of the vortex, a gaping maw of darkness.

I braced myself, expecting we'd plunge into a vast, empty oblivion. We were venturing into the unknown, and I'd be lying if I said I wasn't a little nervous he'd vomit up all that blood he'd just choked down. Trans-dimensional travel was sort of like swimming. Best not attempt it until at least thirty minutes after a meal.

The portal yanked us through in a blur of motion and swirling chaos. My barely beating heart lodged in my throat as we were spat out the other side. I squeezed my eyes shut against the dizzying assault on my senses.

When I opened them again, I found myself standing in the middle of a cornfield, the stalks rising well over my head. A warm sun shone down from a clear blue sky. I blinked in confusion—the sun's rays didn't burn my skin. Somehow, impossibly, I walked under the sun again.

I turned to Muggs. "Are you sure you got the right place? This looks like fucking Nebraska."

Muggs frowned, equally bewildered. "I don't understand. This is the exact dimensional coordinate where the djinn's lamp was sent. But..."

"Something's changed," Jinx finished for him. She surveyed our surroundings, cornstalks whispering in the breeze. "I don't think we're just in another dimension. I think we're inside the lamp itself."

My brows shot up. That... actually made a crazy sort of sense. But it raised a whole new crop of questions.

"How is that possible?" I asked. "The lamp was shattered."

Muggs nodded slowly, piecing it together. "Yes, and the pocket dimension wasn't much. When the lamp was destroyed, the small reality that Adam forged here became a void. But a djinn's lamp always reconstitutes itself after it's destroyed."

I caught on. "So when the lamp reformed..."

"The lamp-world *is* the other dimension, one and the same now," Muggs concluded. "It's certainly going to complicate matters in a hundred years when we have to bring the lamp hope so the djinn can take Ladinas' place."

I shook my head. "One problem at a time. I'm not worried about what we'll have to do in a century. How are we going to bring Ladinas home so we can bring him to Alice?"

Juliet shook her head. "You said it. One problem at a time. We need to find Ladinas. Why would he make a world of cornfields? He didn't strike me as the farming type. Why not forge a world that reminded him of old-world Romania, or a white sand beach, or something... less corny."

I snorted. "Did you really just tell a corny joke... about corn?"

Juliet grimaced. "Yeah. Sorry about that. I don't know what came over me."

I laughed, the bad joke breaking some of the tension I felt. This strange facsimile of a Midwestern farm was unnerving in its normalcy.

"Ladinas always fancied himself a romantic," I mused. "He read those cheesy paperback romances—all secret trysts in moonlit gardens and longing glances across candlelit dinners."

Juliet raised an eyebrow. "Somehow I can't picture our resident ancient badass getting all misty-eyed over a melodramatic love story."

"Oh, you'd be surprised," I said with a grin. "I once caught him reading *Twilight*, of all things. He was utterly engrossed. Said he related to the 'tortured immortal finding meaning in the love of a mortal girl' or some nonsense."

Juliet burst out laughing. "No way! Please tell me you're joking."

I shook my head, chuckling. "Nope, straight truth. He ate those books up. But..." I trailed off, piecing it together.

"What is it?" Juliet asked.

"After Ladinas disappeared, I helped Alice tidy up his room. On his daystand was a copy of *Little House on the Prairie*."

"Huh," Juliet said. "He went from secret vampire-human trysts to life on the wholesome prairie."

Muggs furrowed his brow. "Daystand? What's a daystand?"

I rolled my eyes. "Vampires are nocturnal, Muggs. We sleep during the day, if at all, not at night. So we call them daystands instead of nightstands."

"Ah, right. Vampire semantics," Muggs said.

I nodded. "The point is, we'd been through so much shit that he was dreaming of a simpler, more innocent world. Can't say I blame him."

Juliet scanned our surroundings. "Well, it looks like that's what he got. Doesn't get much simpler than this."

Juliet nodded, then aimed her shotgun at the sky. "Ladinas! Get your undead ass out here! We've come to harsh your mellow!"

She fired. The shotgun blast echoed back at us from a distance.

I chuckled. "Subtle as always, Jinx."

After Juliet's shotgun blast, there was a moment of silence before we heard the rustling of corn stalks nearby. We aimed our weapons at the source, but instead of Ladinas, a young girl emerged from the fields.

She couldn't have been over ten years old, with long black hair and bright blue eyes. Her clothes were tattered and dirty, but she held herself with an air of confidence that seemed out of place in this eerie corn kingdom.

"Who are you?" Juliet asked, her gun still trained on the girl.

The girl didn't seem afraid of our weapons. Instead, she smiled and curtsied. "My name is Beatrice," she said. "I am one of Ladinas's loyal subjects."

Juliet lowered her gun slightly, still wary. "How old are you, Beatrice?"

Beatrice tilted her head. "I don't remember anything before… I think a month ago. Maybe more, maybe less. I'm pretty new."

I sighed. Ladinas hadn't only created a pretend world. He'd populated it, too. But this little girl seemed real and self-aware. What in the world was he thinking? Was he really making a world that he knew would cease to exist when his time in the lamp was over?

I kneeled down and took Beatrice's hands. "Do you know where Ladinas is?"

"Of course!" Beatrice beamed. "Did he make you just now? He's always bringing me new friends. He's so nice, isn't he?"

"Nice." I pressed my lips together. I mean, he wasn't *mean*. 'Nice' just isn't an adjective I'd ever thought to apply to the Vampire Prince. Dark, alluring, seductive. All those descriptors applied. But *nice?* "He didn't make us. But you're right about one thing. We *are* friends."

"Goodie!" Beatrice jumped up and down, her farm dress billowing around her dainty legs. "How about a game of hide and seek?"

Juliet stepped forward. "Take us to your leader."

"Okie doke!" Beatrice giggled. "Follow me!"

As the young girl weaved between the stalks, Muggs held his hand on my shoulder and followed as Juliet and I stayed just a few paces behind Beatrice.

I leaned over toward Juliet. "Take us to your leader? Alien invasion cliché much?"

Juliet snickered. "We *are* aliens if you think about it. Of a sort. What can I say? I've always wanted to say that. The opportunity was there, so I took it."

Chapter 13

An endless sea of cornstalks swayed in the hot summer breeze, swallowing us as we trudged along. The sun beat down on my neck, not that I could feel its heat. My boots crunched on the dusty path as the strange farm girl, Beatrice, led us toward the billowing smokestack in the distance.

We crested a hill, and there it was - the quaint farmhouse Ladinas had crafted in this pocket world. Surrounding it, penned in by makeshift fences, were odd hybrid creatures that resembled warped versions of livestock. Mismatched parts of pigs, chickens, cows, and horses lumbered about, the twisted menagerie of Ladinas's peculiar imagination.

What really caught my eye was the church next to the house, a towering wooden cross perched atop its steeple. "The hell is Ladinas doing with a church?" I muttered. "Mr. 'I'm God of My Own Universe' building shrines to the big guy upstairs? That's a first commandment no-no if I've ever seen one."

Muggs just shrugged, the wisps of his beard fluttering in the breeze. "I'm sure he's got his reasons. No harm in asking."

Beatrice led us inside the farmhouse, the screen door creaking as it swung open. There, sitting by the fire, was Ladinas. Or at least, I thought it was him. Gone was the slick, dark-haired vampire I knew. In his place sat a man who looked exactly like Michael Landon, but with Ladinas' face. Bushy hair curling down to his shoulders, tucked into a wide-brimmed hat. Suspenders over a dusty flannel shirt.

Little House on the goddamn Prairie. I knew it. I'd seen a few episodes of the show. The one thing I didn't remember from it was Frankensteinian farm animals. But as the god of his own lamp realm, Ladinas was entitled to artistic license.

Another weird creature was curled up at his feet. Like a dog, a goat, and a cat, all got shot up with cupid arrows and somehow their genetics got mixed up, they impregnated each other, and produced a single baby.

The damn thing was hideous. But I'd seen worse. Like some human babies. Yeah, some people have really ugly children. Not like I'd ever tell them that. But we all know it when we see it. When someone shows you the pictures of their children and your first thought is, "Damn! What the—"

It's a totally different experience when someone shows you their kittens. There's no such thing as an ugly kitten.

In a way, I supposed, these abominations were Ladinas' ugly kids. Total monstrosities. No one would dispute it. But telling him that required bigger balls than I had in the moment. No reason to take a shit on his personal paradise.

Ladinas blinked in surprise. "Mercy? What are you doing here?" he asked. "It's barely been a few weeks."

I swallowed down my shock, shaking my head. "Doesn't matter. We need your help."

I quickly explained that Oblivion had escaped using cupid magic, possessed Alice, and was wreaking havoc back on Earth.

Ladinas sighed, smoke billowing from his lips. I could see the worry in his eyes, but also a sense of helplessness. "And what is it you want of me?"

"We want you to help us save Alice and the goddamn world," I said bluntly.

But Ladinas shook his head. "I'm still too weak. As a djinn, I won't have enough power to manifest on Earth for a century. I cannot leave permanently until the original djinn returns for his lamp."

Juliet stepped forward, eyes blazing with determination. "That's not entirely true," she said sharply. "If we cast this whole freaky realm into another dimension, where time passes much more quickly than it does on earth, you can draw enough power to return with us."

"Juliet!" I exclaimed. "That would mean doubling Ladinas's sentence to this lamp. He'd have to spend another century just to get strong enough to give us a fool's chance."

Juliet shook her head. "All we have is a fool's chance, Mercy."

"She's right," Ladinas added. "I was willing to endure a hundred years here hoping at the end of it Alice and I could be together. But if I do nothing at all, I'll endure my sentence for nothing. There won't be a world to return to. Alice will be gone, consumed by Oblivion. If I do this, it revives my original hope. One century, then I can be with Alice."

"But we'll still have to deal with Oblivion," I added. "All of this hinges on the vague hope that *maybe* Alice will find the strength to cast Oblivion out of her body when she sees you."

He paused, looking troubled. "If there's any chance at all it will work, I'd wait a thousand years to gain the power necessary, if that's what it took."

Juliet gasped and placed her hand over her mouth. "My god. That's the sweetest thing I've ever heard."

I cocked an eyebrow at Juliet. "Don't tell me you're going to cry."

"No!" Juliet shuddered. "I'm going to vomit. Damn, that's some sappy shit, Ladinas."

Ladinas laughed. "You two really are a couple peas of the same pod."

I took Juliet's hand in mind, our fingers interlacing by habit. "We're happy. Those cupids really screwed with our relationship, but in the end, we both realized that *wanting* to love each other was a lot more important than fleeting passion."

Ladinas smiled widely. "I'm happy for you, Mercy. I'm happy for both of you. I wish I could be there to enjoy this with you."

"We really need to get this plan rolling." I turned to Muggs. "Are you sure you can roll this pocket dimension into another one?"

"Adam would be better suited for the task," Muggs said. "But we've crossed a few dimensions before where we experienced the disjunction in time comparable to what we require. But we'll still need a few days, earth-time, for Ladinas to power up in what will be a century from his perspective."

Ladinas cleared his throat. "I trust you. *All* of you. While you're waiting for me to be ready, all I can say is fight like hell. Do whatever you can to delay Oblivion, and if there's any way to protect Alice in the meantime, do what you might."

I nodded. "We'll come up with something. Hailey might know a few spells that will help distract Oblivion. But holding him off for *days*…well, it won't be easy, but we'll do whatever it takes."

"In that case," Ladinas gestured to Beatrice. "Would you please get our guests a drink?"

"Of course!" Beatrice exclaimed.

I furrowed my brow. "Drinks? We don't drink tea, Ladinas. You realize we're still vampires, right?"

"Three mugs of O-negative coming your way!" Beatrice announced.

I cocked an eyebrow. "You have humans back there bleeding into mugs?"

Ladinas shook his head and flashed a fangy grin. "Not at all! This is my domain, Mercy. Blood flows on tap. The finest you'll ever taste. Trust me."

It only took Beatrice a few seconds. That girl, as young as she was, came with instilled obedience. She was nothing if not efficient. When she returned, three mugs on a single platter, I grabbed mine.

"Thank you, Beatrice."

"My pleasure!" The girl beamed.

We all took our first sips at the same time. "Damn!" My eyes shot wide. "This is delicious!"

I hadn't seen such an impassioned look on Juliet's face since the last time we slept together—before all this cupid shit got in the way of things. "It's amazing."

Muggs chugged his entire mug and belched, leaving a crimson mustache on his upper lip.

Juliet snickered. "Got blood?"

"Told you," Ladinas smirked. "You couldn't get blood this pure if you fed from a convent."

I laughed and shook my head. "Speaking of convents. What's up with the church? You suddenly decide to find religion while you're trapped in the lamp?"

Ladinas shrugged. "You know Alice. She's the only vampire I've ever known who has kept her faith over more than a century of existence. I admire that about her. I figured, you know, if I could find a little religion while I was here, maybe it would be something we could share when I returned."

I glanced at Juliet. If she was about to vomit at Ladinas' sappiness before, this would put her over the top. But Juliet was so enthralled by her mug full of mystically conjured O-negative to notice. I turned back to Ladinas. "I think that's amazing. I never thought I'd be able to bring myself to admit it, but you and Alice... you deserve each other."

Chapter 14

I TOOK IN A deep breath of the pure cornfield air and took a final mental note, appreciating the heat of the sun blazing overhead. The farmhouse stood behind us, Ladinas and Beatrice inside. I hated leaving him behind. The whole notion of consigning him to an extra century was almost too much to bear, but it was necessary and he was willing. I could only pray to gods I didn't really trust that this plan would work. I'd come up with a lot of long shot plans through the years. Some of them even worked—though those that did usually came with a hitch or two I hadn't expected.

The only thing I knew to expect if this was going to work was that *something* unexpected was going to make this even harder than it already was.

Mugs spun his staff overhead, emerald magic flowing from the tips into a vortex. "There's one last thing I must do before we leave. I'll have to send you both back first."

My guts twisted. "What? Why?"

"To move Ladinas' entire realm, I must cast the spell from within while encompassing the borders. It's the only way."

I grabbed Muggs' arm. "But if you trap yourself in there, how will you return to our time?"

Muggs patted my hand reassuringly. "Not to worry, love. Time flows faster in the other dimension. I should be back in your time almost instantly after you two reappear."

I chewed my lip, uncertain. "And if your spell fails? If the realm you're planning to use isn't there anymore? What if you don't return quickly?"

Muggs sighed. "Use a convergence. Flee the earth. Save yourselves and screw everyone else."

I rolled my eyes. "That's not funny. I'm serious."

"So am I. Because if something happens that gets in my way, you'll either need to come up with some other way to beat Oblivion without me or leave the earth and find another world to call home." He squeezed my shoulder. "But I promise, all will go as planned."

Muggs didn't make many promises. He knew better. When magic was involved, there were always complications or extenuating circumstances. If he was so certain, this time, I had to believe it would work.

"Alright," I shook my head. "But moving one dimension into another doesn't sound *easy*."

Muggs shrugged. "It isn't. But I know what I'm doing."

Juliet squeezed my hand. What did I really have to worry about? My gut told me something was about to go awry. I just didn't know what.

Muggs spun his staff overhead, conjuring a swirling green vortex. As it descended over us, I squeezed Juliet's hand back tightly. A flash of light, a stomach-dropping sensation of falling, and we slammed back into reality, stumbling onto the cold concrete floor of one of the hallways in the Underground.

I took a deep breath, steadying myself against the wall. "We're home."

Before I could fully process our return, Muggs appeared with a pop and another green flash, grinning widely. "Told you I'd be right behind you."

I tilted my head, studying him closely. "So everything went smoothly? Where exactly did you send Ladinas?"

"A realm you've never seen," Muggs said vaguely. He leaned on his staff. "I've explored many dimensions over the centuries."

I crossed my arms. "Well, don't keep me in suspense. What's this one like? Is it safe?"

Muggs chuckled. "Oh, it's a silly place. All pastel colors and singing ponies." He waved a hand. "You know, where friendship is magic."

I stared at him. "Seriously? That's an actual realm?"

"Gods no," Muggs laughed. "That's just a cartoon. I sent them to Smurf Village."

I stared at Muggs, unamused. "Come on, enough messing around. Where did you really send them?"

Muggs held up his hands in surrender. "Alright, alright. I discovered an empty dimension ages ago. Nothing of note there, just endless pancakes as far as the eye can see."

Jinx snickered. "The Kingdom of Mrs. Butterworth?"

"Exactly!" Muggs grinned. "Though Aunt Jemima is vying for control of their sugary sweet empire."

I rolled my eyes. "We don't have time for jokes. We need to find Hailey and the others, figure out how to slow Oblivion down. Somehow, we have to preserve the world for a few days until Ladinas is strong enough to help."

Muggs nodded, his expression growing serious. "You're right. I'm sorry. It wasn't pancakes. It was waffles. But Mrs. Butterworth is just as good there as she is in any breakfast dimension."

We ventured deeper into the Underground, our footsteps echoing through the empty tunnels. Unease prickled my skin. This place was never totally abandoned—there were always a few vampires milling about. But now, only silence.

Jinx voiced my thoughts aloud. "Where the hell is everyone?"

I quickened my pace, dread pooling in my stomach. The control room, the dorms—all deserted. Even Clement and the orphans were gone without a trace.

I met Jinx's worried gaze. "Something happened while we were away. This is Oblivion's doing."

Just as I thought my stomach was about to fall out of my ass, a flash of rainbow light filled the room. Pauli appeared right on my shoulders.

"Eeek! Damn it! Get off me!"

"Hey hoes and bros!" Pauli announced. "Sorry to startle you, but... well... to quote the Arnold..."

"Get to the chopper?" Juliet asked.

"Come with me if you want to live?" I guessed. "What happened here, Pauli?"

"It's not a tumor?" Muggs chimed in. It didn't make a damn bit of sense, but whatever.

"Hasta la vista, bitches!" Pauli announced, ignoring my question. Then, expanding his serpentine length around all three of us, in another flash of multicolored light, we were gone.

Chapter 15

THE SENSATION OF BEING squeezed through a tube hit me as the colors of Pauli's scales blurred before my eyes. A second later, the pressure released and I stumbled forward onto soft, mossy ground. Muggs and Juliet collapsed with me in a tangle of limbs.

Druid teleportation was jarring. Pauli's methods were just as disorienting.

I inhaled deeply, the earthy aroma of the forest filling my lungs. Towering pines surrounded us, leaves and branches filtering the moonlight in patches on the forest floor.

"What happened? Why are we hiding out in the middle of nowhere?" I asked, steadying myself against a lichen-speckled tree trunk.

I'd barely steadied myself when a three-hundred pound ball of fur collided with me. My face was soon drowning in hellhound tongue. Call it a poor-girl's facial. "Goliath!"

Speaking the dog's name didn't slow him down. He was *that* happy to see me. We might have lost most of our team, but at least my hell dog was safe.

Hailey and Mel emerged from behind a thicket of brambles. I managed to squeeze myself out from under Goliath's massive frame and calmed him down with a few strategic behind-the-ear scratches. "Are we all that's left?"

Hailey nodded to Mel, who handed me a tablet displaying security footage from the Underground. "You need to see this. It will explain everything."

My stomach twisted as I examined the security recordings.

Alice writhed on the screen, her skin covered in dark scales, an aura of nothingness radiating from her. She breathed on the vampires around her and they vanished, consumed by her breath, disappearing into oblivion.

I watched Antoine evaporate before my eyes. Another feed showed Clement shielding the orphans, all of them blinking out of existence as Alice vomited her void ichor over them.

"I tried to fight her." Hailey's voice was laced with defeat. "But Oblivion absorbed my blood magic. Everything I threw at them only made them stronger."

Mel added, "We had no choice but to flee. Pauli brought us here."

I nodded, still processing the loss. "Hiding outdoors isn't wise. We're vampires. We'll need shelter before sunrise."

Mel gestured to a craggy ridge in the distance. "There's a cave system over that rise we can use come morning. Pauli and Muggs can teleport back for the kevlar suits if we end up needing them."

She glanced down at her tablet. "At least out here I'm still getting a signal. I've been monitoring the security feeds."

I raised an eyebrow, prompting her to continue.

"We had Pauli grab you, Jinx, and Muggs as soon as you returned to the Underground," she explained. "Didn't want to risk Alice catching your scent."

My fists clenched at the mention of Alice's name. She'd been my nemesis for most of our existence, but now ... whatever she used to be, no matter our past issues, she didn't deserve this—twisted and defiled by Oblivion's possession.

I took a deep, unnecessary breath to steady myself. There would be time to mourn later. Right now, we needed to focus.

"Any luck reaching Ladinas?" Hailey asked, a glimmer of hope in her voice.

I shook my head. "We have a plan, but it's going to take a few days. Muggs has shifted Ladinas' lamp into a pocket dimension where time moves faster relative to our world. But even then…"

Muggs picked up my trailing thought. "Ladinas is stuck in the lamp. He's functioning as a djinn, but he won't have enough power to manifest on earth for decades, close to a century. Even with the disjunction in time between dimensions, though, he won't be strong enough to manifest for at least two or three days, our time."

I met Hailey's gaze. "And that's assuming the plan even works. Ladinas might show up and Alice might breathe him straight out of existence. Just like everyone else…"

She nodded, processing this. After a moment, she added, "We don't know for sure that's what happened to them. This isn't like any magic I've ever encountered, and there aren't many witches who've dabbled in more than I have. But even magic—all magic—follows certain laws within the material world. Matter, energy, spirits, whatever. They can't just cease to be. Their energy has to exist in some form, somewhere. But we're dealing with something way beyond earthly magic. When you were bound to Oblivion, could he just breathe shit out of being?"

I thought back to my own brush with the entity. "He had a different strategy with me. Seduction, manipulation. But even then, Oblivion never displayed an ability to outright erase things from existence." I shook my head. "If he could have done that, I would have known."

Mel's eyes widened with desperate hope. "Then our friends are out there somewhere. We just have to save them."

I rubbed my brow, considering. "When Oblivion possessed me, I also had Caladbolg within me. The two referred to themselves as Calivion. My emotions gave Oblivion's nature more influence, but I think Caladbolg's essence still restrained some of his abilities."

Hailey sighed. "So it might be that Oblivion can do things with Alice he could never do through you."

I met Hailey's gaze. "I'm afraid so. With no counterbalance, Alice could be far more dangerous under Oblivion's thrall than I ever was."

Muggs pinched his chin thoughtfully. "Oblivion is the antithesis of Caladbolg, correct? The dragons were the original gatekeepers, the guardians of existence. Before, Oblivion could only manipulate the gates and convergences. But now..."

"Now he can create them," Hailey finished grimly. "The dragons weren't just guardians of the realms. They were the sentinels of existence itself. Without them maintaining universal balance..."

Muggs nodded. "There cannot be light without darkness. For every power, there must exist its opposite."

Juliet stepped forward, determination in her eyes. "I wasn't here when you battled Oblivion before. But if anyone knows what truly happened to the others, it's Alice.

We have to stick to the plan—buy time for Ladinas until we can reach her."

She placed a hand on my shoulder. "I know it's hard, but we can't focus on rescuing them now. We have to trust that if they still exist, we'll learn the truth and save them when this is over."

I met her steadfast gaze and nodded. "You're right. If we fail, nothing will exist any more anyway. Including our friends."

Hailey bit her lip. "But how do we restrain Oblivion? My blood magic only strengthens him."

I considered this. "Then we don't use blood magic. If Caladbolg was Oblivion's counterbalance, we need something to stand in and do the same job. We need a magic that represents the opposite of everything Oblivion is about. Magic that honors existence, nature itself. We need you, Muggs."

Muggs inclined his head. "Druidic magic may be our best shot. But it won't be easy. And if I'm shot again..." He left the thought unfinished, rubbing his right glute where he was shot before. Then he threw his voice into his best Forrest Gump impression. "I got shot. In the buttocks."

"And you thought you were in love with me." Mel shook her head.

"You know the way to a man's heart," Pauli smirked. "It's up the ass!"

I pushed my lips together in a futile attempt to hold back a laugh. I wasn't in the mood for jokes, but honestly, I needed a little humor at the moment. Without it, I might have unraveled.

"Muggs is our best shot to hold Oblivion back until Ladinas is ready. Besides, we'll need Muggs to retrieve Ladians when the time comes. Whatever else is going on, we can't let anything happen to Muggs."

"My blood magic may not be useful against Oblivion," Hailey said, "but my shields can protect you while you cast, Muggs."

Muggs nodded, his brow furrowed in thought. "I know a few spells that may help restrain him, at least for a time." He met my gaze. "But I cannot guarantee they will hold Oblivion for long. His power is ancient, primal—chaos given form."

"We only need to restrain him long enough to enact our plan," I said. Though doubt gnawed at me, I kept my tone confident. "If anyone can weave the magic to bind a force like Oblivion, even briefly, it's you, Muggs."

Juliet stepped closer to Muggs and gripped his arm. "We have faith in you," she said softly. Hailey nodded agreement.

Muggs patted Juliet's hand; resolve hardening his features. "Then I will do all I can. The risk is great, but as you say, we have little left to lose at this point except existence itself." He attempted a wry smile. "And I've grown rather fond of existing, truth be told."

Despite everything, I huffed a laugh. "That makes two of us. We'll stand together, come what may." I met each of their eyes in turn, seeing my own staunch determination reflected back. "We won't go down without a hell of a fight."

Chapter 16

I CLOSED MY EYES and took a deep breath, the fate of the world resting heavily on my shoulders. Muggs may be a blind, quirky, OnlyFans foot modeling druid, but he was reliable when it mattered most. We'd stop Oblivion's madness or die trying.

"We need to figure out Oblivion's next move," Hailey said, breaking the tense silence.

Mel's fingers flew across her tablet as she searched for any scrap of intel, but came up empty. "I've got nothing. Zero chatter on the police scanners."

I sighed. "Well, when Oblivion was using me, we paid the cops a visit. A total power play. This time, though. If they did the same, there might not be any police left."

The rising sun split the tree line, casting fingers of light across the forest floor. We were running out of time. "We can't let that monster run free all day without making our move. We can take shelter in the caves for now. But we can't wait the day out. We need kevlar."

Hailey shook her head. "Wouldn't it be best if Oblivion and Alice aren't doing anything to alert us to their activities to just let them be? We only need a couple of days."

"Too risky," I said. "The one thing I know about Oblivion is that he doesn't take breaks. If he isn't doing anything we know about, he's planning something, preparing for something big. I'm not of a mind to wait for him to strike to make our move. Whatever he's going to do next will surely be deadly, and probably catastrophic."

"Then how do we find him?" Mel asked. "Once we go into those caves, I'll lose service. So unless he shows himself on something I can track in the next few minutes before the sun is up, we won't know where to look."

I twirled my wand between my fingers. "The best way to find Oblivion will be to give him what he wants. When he used me, he drew on my deepest seated resentments. I know Alice and I have tolerated one another in recent years, but deep down, she spent most of her life trying to kill me. She still blames me, at some level, for becoming a vampire. Not to mention, Oblivion and I have our own issues. Although he doesn't have the use of me anymore, he still sees me as a threat. That's why he came after the Underground. Bottom line, if they have a chance, they'll come after me."

Juliet's eyes widened. "Please tell me you're not considering offering yourself up as dragon bait."

I set my jaw. "If we can't find him, we may have no choice."

"We still have to know where to fish," Muggs added. "You can't just drop bait anywhere and expect a bite."

I shrugged. "Then we go where the cupids have concentrated their efforts all this time. They still flow with his power. If one of them sees me, he'll know it."

"The Ridley Hotel," Mel sighed. "I'm really beginning to hate that place. But you'll still need kevlar. The sunlight is already searing our skin."

"Everyone inside," I said. "Paulie, can you handle retrieving the kevlar? We can't risk Muggs right now. He's too pivotal to the plan."

"But Pauli is expendable? You bitch!" Even with a boa constrictor's face, I could see his smirk shining through.

"Yup. That's me. But the bottom line, Pauli, is that risking Muggs right now risks all of us. We need you to do this."

Pauli's forked tongue fluttered in the air. "I get it. I can handle it. Enough suits for everyone?"

"Should be," Mel added. "Hailey should fit in Alice's suit. It's in her locker."

Pauli disappeared in a flash. The rest of us headed into the caves, the cool air a welcome respite. The real sun was a lot less pleasant than the one Ladinas made in his lamp world.

Juliet sat down beside me on a slick rock, leaning her head on my shoulder. We didn't say anything. We just existed—together—for a few minutes. Sometimes that's all you can really do—exist with someone. Just *be*. It meant more than words. It gave me a strength, a resolve, I didn't realize I needed.

How often do we go about our existence, bitching and moaning about shit that doesn't matter in the grand scheme of things? We take life—existence—for granted every day.

We were *literally* a dragon's breath away from ceasing to be. The entire world was teetering on the brink of the void.

A few minutes later, Pauli reappeared in a flash, his serpentine body coiled around a giant bag filled with our black kevlar sun-proof suits.

"Pauli's back, bitches! Time to suit up and kick some ass."

We quickly got dressed. The tight material clung to every curve and contour. I couldn't help but admire how sexy Juliet looked, even as she grumbled about her piercings getting caught in the fabric.

"There's only one problem with trying to attract Oblivion at the hotel," Muggs said. "My magic flows from the earth. The deeper in the city we are, the weaker I'll be."

"Right. So maybe start at the hotel. All I need is one of those damn cupids to see me. If I get their attention, I can lead them out toward the woods. Oblivion won't be far behind."

It wasn't a bad idea. Except for one problem.

"Oblivion can fly," Hailey pointed out. "He'll be able to chase you through the air while you're stuck on the ground."

"Not necessarily," Pauli said. "I can teleport her around, keep her just ahead of them but not close enough for them to actually reach."

Hailey looked eager. "I should come too, help run interference--"

Pauli shook his head. "It'll be harder to 'port more than one person. You, Mel and Jinx need to stay with Muggs, keep him safe until it's time."

Hailey nodded in agreement. "You're probably right. I just hate dangling Mercy out there like that."

I put my hand on her shoulder. "Right now, I'm more expendable than Muggs. And with Pauli moving me ahead of Oblivion, we should be able to lure him right into our trap."

"I know." She gave me a quick hug. "Just be careful."

No sooner did Hailey release me and a tug on my arm spun me around. Juliet pulled me close and kissed me, soft and fierce. "Don't do anything too stupidly heroic, okay?"

"I'll try to resist," I said dryly.

Juliet smiled, her eyes full of emotion. "I mean it. Come back to me in one piece."

I nodded, not trusting my voice. Then Pauli slithered up my body to wrap loosely around my shoulders. His tongue flicked out, tickling my ear.

"Cut it out," I said, twitching away.

Pauli hissed out a chuckle. Leave it to Pauli to find the worst moment to be annoying as fuck.

"Let's do this," I ordered. "Back to Ridley Hotel."

Pauli's grip around me tightened. The world blinked out for a split second, replaced by the downtown street outside the hotel turned cupid lair. It was just past dawn, but the streets were devoid of the usual rush-hour hubbub. Between the cupids and their chaos, and Oblivion's return, Providence was a ghost town. In a more literal way than I wanted to admit.

I took a deep breath, steadying myself. "Time to hook the worm."

Pauli shuddered, his body trembling over my shoulders. "That sounds painful! Don't hook my worm!"

I rolled my eyes. "I'm not talking about your penis, Pauli."

"Better not be! Because I don't have a worm. I have an anaconda!"

I furrowed my brow. "You're a boa constrictor, with an anaconda for a penis?"

"When I'm in human form, duh! Snakes aren't well hung. Or are we? Maybe all we are is… one massive…"

"Can we change the subject, please? As fascinated as you are by the size of your own snakehood, we have a goddamn dragon to catch."

Chapter 17

THE STENCH OF STALE sweat, blood, and sex assaulted my nostrils as we crept through the dimly lit corridors of the Ridley Hotel. Pauli bobbed his head as he dangled from my shoulders. "I smell sex and caaandy..."

I clamped my hand over his mouth. "Shut it, unless you want to announce our presence to every Cupid in the vicinity."

He wrenched himself free. "That's the whole point! We're trying to get their attention, remember?"

"Well, can you find a less irritating way to help? Besides, I don't smell any candy here at all."

"But you do smell the sex!" He cackled. I rolled my eyes, even though he was right. This place had been one massive orgy on our last visit.

We slunk into the ballroom, where all hell had broken loose before. Where Oblivion had abandoned my body and possessed Alice instead. The expansive room now sat empty and silent, but something prickled my witch senses. I felt the hairs on my neck stand up as I detected a strange magic.

"Do you feel that?" I murmured. Pauli shook his head, oblivious. I followed the unsettling energy to a small kitchen area behind the ballroom. The tiles had been blasted apart, revealing a gaping hole with a massive convergence swirling inside—a vortex leading to another world.

The dark tendrils of the portal twisted and curled like living shadows. I'd never seen magic like this before.

"Where do you think that goes?" Pauli whispered, uncharacteristically serious.

I shook my head. "We suspected there might be some kind of gate here. My guess is it connects to whatever world the Cupids came from."

"But aren't cupids creatures of chaos and servants of Oblivion? Wouldn't they have come from the void—from non-existence itself?"

"I don't know," I admitted. "Just because they enjoy chaos doesn't mean they come from the void. Oblivion could have recruited the little bastards from God knows where."

Pauli chewed his lip. "Do you think Oblivion and Alice could be hiding on whatever world is on the other side? Gathering an army or something to launch a final attack?"

My stomach knotted. "It's not just possible, it's likely. And if Oblivion still has the rest of the Underground captive, that's probably where they are, too."

I stared into the swirling vortex, considering our options. This changed everything.

"The magic here definitely resembles Alice's breath," Pauli said. Well, Oblivion's breath. Unless she had a habit of eating life-destroying ass before Oblivion possessed her."

I furrowed my brow. "Life-destroying ass? I don't even know what that means."

Pauli shook his snake-shaped head. "When all this is over, I'll tell you all about my *last* Friday. I mean, he was cute, right? So I figured he'd be clean, neat, ready for a Pauli Pounding. But good lord. Ever hear of manscaping? He sure hadn't. That's for damn sure."

I pressed my lips together. "A Pauli Pounding?"

"It's trademarked, bitch. Don't use it or I'll sue your cold, dead ass."

I rolled my eyes. I wasn't in the mood for Pauli's shit. "I think you can keep that story to yourself. Whatever's going on here, it changes our plans."

Pauli flicked his forked tongue, tasting the air near the portal. "I wonder if I could sneak through and do a little recon without being noticed."

"Too dangerous," I said firmly. "We do not know what's on the other side. I won't risk you getting hurt or trapped there."

Pauli sighed but didn't argue. He stepped back from the vortex, preparing to teleport us out.

But before he could, dark tendrils lashed out from the portal and coiled around my body. I cried out in shock as they yanked me toward the opening.

"Mercy!" Pauli tightened his coil around my wrist, trying to pull me back. I felt his magic swell as he attempted to teleport us both to safety. But a surge of... darkness, of nothingness... flowed through me and repelled his magic.

"It's no use," Pauli hissed. "I can't break its hold on you."

The portal's pull strengthened. Pauli's grip was tight, but I could tell he was losing the tug-of-war match over my body. Our eyes met, and in that moment, I knew what had to happen.

"Go," I told him. "Get back to the others. Warn Hailey what's happened."

"No!" Pauli cried. "I won't leave you!"

"You have to," I said firmly. "They need to know. Please."

Pauli's slitted eyes bored into mine. Then, with a hiss, he released my hand. The tendrils dragged me backwards into the swirling abyss. Pauli's colorful face was the last thing I saw before the void consumed me.

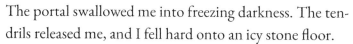

The portal swallowed me into freezing darkness. The tendrils released me, and I fell hard onto an icy stone floor.

Groaning, I pushed myself up and took in my surroundings. I was in a vast cavern dimly lit by glowing crystals jutting from the walls and ceiling. The air was frigid and stale. In the distance, I could hear the echo of dripping water.

I got to my feet, wincing. Nothing seemed broken, but I'd have some nasty bruises later. If there was a later.

I glanced around for an exit but saw only endless, twisting tunnels branching off from the cavern. Shivering, I hugged my arms around myself. My breath misted in front of me.

"Well Mercy," I muttered, "you wanted to find Oblivion. Looks like you got your wish."

The portal was still overhead, but I'd fallen so far that even with my vampiric abilities, there was no way to reach it. I tried to climb the walls, but they were too slick. I couldn't make it more than a few feet up before I slid back to the cold cavern floor.

At least the crystals offered *some* kind of light. What magic powered them? Was it magic at all? I sensed nothing I could use.

Picking a tunnel at random, I started walking. The glowing crystals cast just enough light to see by. The tunnel sloped gradually downward, deeper into the frozen earth.

I quickened my pace, both to warm up and to get somewhere faster. The cold bit at me even through my kevlar. I couldn't stop shivering.

What did I know about this place? Absolutely nothing. I *guessed* that Oblivion and Alice were there, and maybe my friends from the Underground. But I didn't know for sure.

I wasn't even totally sure that this was where the cupids came from. Convergences can change, they can shift. Oblivion could manipulate them. Just because the convergence at Ridley Hotel might have once brought the cupids to our world didn't mean that's where it took me.

But I had to start somewhere. I had to find answers and rescue my friends if they were here. And perhaps, just maybe, put an end to Oblivion once and for all.

As I ventured deeper into the tunnel, the air grew colder and the crystals dimmer. The walls became more jagged, as if nature itself had torn through the earth—or whatever world I was in—to create this labyrinthine underworld.

The sound of dripping water grew louder, echoing through the tunnels like a haunting melody. I deduced that there must be an underground river nearby. Water often led to civilization, right? Or at least something other than this desolate, frozen wasteland.

I followed the sound and eventually came upon a small subterranean river flowing swiftly through the jagged rocks. The water was crystal clear, but it radiated an icy chill.

Bending down, I dipped my hand into the freezing water. It sent a shockwave of cold up my arm, but it didn't harm me.

That convergence pulled me in here... that means someone or something wanted me here.

The thought was jarring. If this was Oblivion's base, if he and Alice were here, somewhere, plotting how they were going to unwind all of my world's existence, they surely knew I was there now. They *wanted* me there.

I stood up, my hand still dripping with the chilling water. Determination surged through me, replacing the fear that threatened to consume me. I couldn't let the unknown overwhelm me. I had faced countless enemies before and came out victorious. This would be no different.

Taking a deep breath, I followed the course of the river, using it as a guide through the winding tunnels. The echoes of my footsteps reverberated off the walls, creating an eerie symphony in this desolate place.

As I walked, I noticed subtle vibrations beneath my feet. The ground trembled slightly, as if there was some kind of immense power coursing through this hidden realm. It sent shivers down my spine, but I pressed on.

Suddenly, a faint glow caught my attention up ahead. Excitement surged within me as I quickened my pace. The glow grew brighter, illuminating the path before me.

Rounding a bend in the tunnel, I stood on the edge of a vast underground lake. The source of the icy river I'd found before.

As I approached the pool, I could feel the power emanating from it. It was so clear that while it might have been a hundred feet deep; it looked as though I could have reached in and touched the bottom. But it was what I saw at the bottom that sent shockwaves through my body.

The djinn's lamp. Ladinas's lamp. Was *this* the world Muggs took it to? If that was the case, why was the convergence at the Ridley Hotel linked to it?

"You think you're so clever…"

The voice startled me so much I nearly slipped into the water. When I whipped around, Alice was staring back at me, Oblivion's darkness filling her eyes and his scales covering her skin.

"What did you do? How did you get here?"

Oblivion laughed through Alice's chapped lips. "I am a dragon, Mercy! Did you really think I wouldn't sense where you went before? Wherever that druid's portals took you?"

I clenched my fists. "You won't get away with this."

Oblivion laughed. "But I already did! You remember the good times we shared, don't you, Mercy?"

I rolled my eyes. "The *good* times? You used me, you son of a bitch."

"Perhaps I did. But you *liked it.* All those people we killed together. For once, you were free. You embraced your true nature. You were a vampire unfettered by the echoes of your pathetic humanity."

"I don't understand. Why did you bring me here, Oblivion? You know I'll never give in to you again."

"I came to make you an offer," Oblivion said. "I might be powerful, but if you'll remember, I was always happy to give you exactly what you wanted in exchange for full access to your... abilities..."

"You made a deal with Alice. She wanted Ladinas back ..."

"And who do you think she blames for his loss? For consigning him to a century in a djinn's lamp?"

I narrowed my eyes. "You aren't as in control of all this shit as you'd like me to believe."

Oblivion shook Alice's head. "My victory is inevitable. You cannot defeat me."

"Then why did you bring me here? You have the lamp. Or do you? Because there's magic in this water. I can feel it. You can't get to it, can you?"

"Your druid progeny was clever. I'll give him that. He enchanted these waters to protect the lamp. I cannot retrieve it without his aid."

I shrugged. "Well, he's not here. And besides. Why do you *need* to give this to Alice, anyway? She's still resisting you, isn't she? She's fighting against your influence."

Oblivion crossed Alice's arms and turned her back to me. "She is compliant. Did I not also promise you everything, Mercy? I'm more than a destroyer. I'm also a lover."

I huffed. "Bullshit. You never loved me. You only promised me what you thought you could use to make me do what you wanted. If the stick doesn't work, you dangle the carrot. Well, I didn't bite. And if Alice knows what's good for her, she won't either."

"But she already has!" Oblivion looked at me with a smile so sinister Alice couldn't have made it herself. "When we found where your druid hid the lamp, and discovered we could not access it, who do you think came up with the plan to lure you here?"

"What the fuck are you talking about?"

"We took your friends!" Oblivion laughed maniacally. "That's your weakness, isn't it? You'll always come for your friends. Even if you have to risk the entire world for their sake. I mean, we'd hoped to capture your druid, but when we realized that wasn't happening..."

"I don't understand." I shook my head. "None of this tracks. When Muggs sent us back to the Underground from the lamp realm, he took care of business and showed up seconds later. You'd *already* attacked our friends."

Oblivion laughed. "Because I've been a dozen steps ahead of you all this time! Do you think I wasn't watching you the whole time you were in the lamp, watching, waiting for you to make a move? I guessed your druid might not be keen to leave the lamp unguarded in this dimension. I knew we'd need leverage. So, before he even brought the lamp here, Alice and I paid your friends a little visit."

"And you *breathed* them away... where are they, Oblivion?"

"When I get the lamp, I'll release your friends. A simple trade."

I crossed my arms. "So you can earn Alice's trust, so she owes you, so you can use her totally and finally destroy our world? I don't think so, scales!"

"You intend to call my bluff, Mercy? Do you think that's wise when the existence of your friends hangs in the balance?"

I took a hard step forward. "I'll tell you what I think. I think you have nothing but a goddamn pair of deuces in your hand and you think you can manipulate me when I'm the one holding the aces. You need me, and you as much as admitted it. You can't make Alice do what you want, and you can't give her what she wants without my help. Well, I can't help you either. Not without Muggs. But here's the truth..."

I gulped. If I told Oblivion this, I really *was* calling his bluff. Everything hinged on my faith in... Alice of all people. "Ladinas agreed to come here, to spend a century in the lamp on another world so that he could finally be powerful enough to be with *you*, Alice, at the end of it."

Alice's lip quivered. Her hard gaze softened. She was in there. I knew it...

"He loves you, Alice. And we're fighting like hell to free you from Oblivion so you can be with Ladinas. You two are meant to be. It's always been the case. And damn it, Alice. I'm sorry I tried to get in between you two. I'm sorry I was jealous. What you two have is real and if you can fight this bastard... I promise... I'll fight or die trying to bring you and Ladinas back together."

Alice's eyes flickered with recognition and a glimmer of hope. The darkness that shrouded her receded, revealing her true self. "Mercy," she choked out, tears streaming down her face.

She whipped around, hiding her face behind her hands. When she turned back to me, her familiar countenance was replaced with rage. "How dare you!" Oblivion screamed. "You try my immortal patience! If you will not do as I demand, I told you the cost! And I'm going to make you watch, so your friends know it was your insolence that killed them!"

Oblivion's voice rose in a furious scream. "How dare you defy me! You are testing my eternal patience! If you refuse to comply with my demands, then you have been warned of the consequences! And I will make sure that your friends watch as your insolence brings about their demise!"

I narrowed my eyes. "You can stop this, Alice. I know you can."

The next thing I knew, the back of her hand struck my cheek. Alice was as strong as me already. With Oblivion in her, it was like someone had driven a bus into the side of my face.

I stumbled backwards, stunned by the blow. My ears were ringing, and my vision was blurry. Oblivion was cackling with malicious delight, but Alice's eyes were still filled with pain.

"If I can't stop you, Alice will!" I spat, trying to gather my wits.

"I'm not Alice anymore," Oblivion snarled. There was no trace of her former humanity or even vampirism left in her voice, but she was in there. I could see it in her eyes. "I am chaos! I am Oblivion!"

My face burned as if the last strike had ripped my flesh from bone. Maybe it had. But I stood strong. Oblivion talked a big game, but his anger betrayed his fear. His pompousness was a thin veneer meant to disguise his weakness.

"I won't let you hurt my friends," I insisted. "And Alice won't let you do it, either."

Oblivion released a deep growl from his throat. "We'll see about that. In the meantime, let's see how much longer your world can survive my cupids."

With a flourish of his hand, a thousand more winged bastards—more than I'd seen before—blasted through the room with quivers on their backs, bows in their hands.

"I might not be able to destroy your world completely without Alice's compliance," Oblivion admitted. "But when my children are done sowing their chaos, will your world be worth saving at all?"

Chapter 18

THE LAST CUPID FLUTTERED away, disappearing into the shadows of the cavern. I watched it go, a knot forming in my stomach.

Muggs, you'd better stick to the plan, I thought to myself. *Don't get distracted by these cupids.*

Oblivion's laughter echoed off the cavern walls. "Come along, Mercy. Wouldn't want you to miss the show."

I squared my shoulders and turned to face him. Alice's body was merely a puppet; the thing controlling her was ancient, cruel. "You won't lay a finger on them," I said. "Not if you want my help to get the djinn's lamp."

"Oh, but plans change, darling. I don't need your help anymore." Oblivion examined Alice's nails with a bored expression. "I'll unravel this puny world with or without you. But for now, I think I'll have some fun erasing your friends from existence."

My fists clenched. I longed to wipe that smug look off Alice's face, but Oblivion would just toss me aside like a rag doll. "So that's it? What about our deal?"

"That ship has sailed, I'm afraid." Oblivion pushed past me, heading for the cavern exit. "The stakes have risen! What I want now isn't the lamp…"

I hurried after him, my mind racing. There had to be some way to stall him, to buy us more time. But Oblivion was hellbent on destruction, drunk on his own power.

"Then what *do* you want?! What will you take to stop this madness?"

Oblivion ignored my question. He continued down the winding cavern path, whistling an eerie, off-key tune. The sound grated on my nerves, echoing off the walls and amplifying until it felt like nails on a chalkboard.

I lunged, trying to tackle Oblivion from behind, but he flung out a hand and I slammed into the cavern wall. The impact knocked the wind out of me. As I struggled back to my feet, Oblivion glanced over his shoulder, an amused glint in his eye.

"Nice try, but you can't stop me that easily."

"Why won't you tell me what you want?!"

Oblivion chuckled and went back to his infuriating whistling as he continued down the path.

Soon we emerged into a massive cavern, the ceiling soaring up into darkness. The walls were coated with a shimmering ichor. Small cocoons... containing my friends... stuck to the walls.

Antoine, Clement, the orphans, even some of Juliet's younglings. They looked like grotesque mummies, insects caught in a spider's web...

Oblivion sauntered up to one of the ichor pods and wiped a section clean, revealing the soldier inside. My throat tightened. "Don't... please..."

But Oblivion just smiled, placing a hand on the vampire's forehead. In the blink of an eye, he was gone. No breath. No flash of energy. Just... gone.

"Bye bye, bloodsucker!" Oblivion cackled.

He went from pod to pod, casually wiping vampires out of existence. I clawed at his back. I screamed for him to stop, but he ignored me.

I pleaded with Alice to fight back, to stop Oblivion from using her body for such evil. But she remained motionless, Oblivion's possession absolute.

Finally, he paused and turned back to me, a wicked grin on his face. "There's the Mercy I know. Such delicious anger simmering inside you."

He leaned in close, his breath hot on my face. "I'll stop, but only if you let me in. Let me take away all that pain."

A shiver went through me. I realized then what he was trying to do - stoke my rage, my sorrow, to worm his way back into my mind. With my powers as a witch, I was the one he truly craved to control.

I took a deep breath, steadying myself. "Just... just don't hurt anyone else. Please."

Oblivion laughed, a harsh sound like nails on slate. "You can't bargain with me, witch. I'll do as I please. But it's cute that you think you can."

He turned and wiped the ichor away from Antoine's pod. My friend's face emerged, lifeless.

"This one is loyal to you, no?" Oblivion sneered. "It would be a shame if something happened to him."

Fury boiled up inside me. "Don't you fucking dare!" I snarled. But even as the words left my mouth, I felt my control slipping. Oblivion's manipulation was working.

I had to stay calm. I couldn't give him the foothold he wanted inside my mind. But with Antoine's life on the line, I didn't know if I could...

Oblivion's eyes glinted with malicious glee. "Let go, Mercy. Or your friend will pay the price."

I took a deep breath, steadying myself. "You feed on our emotions," I said evenly. "That's all you have left to cling to. All you can use to manipulate us."

I met Alice's gaze, trying to reach the friend trapped within. "Don't let him poison you with anger and pain, Alice. You're stronger than he is."

Oblivion threw back his head and cackled. "That's the problem with you pathetic creatures. You're more like the humans you feed from than you care to admit. Ruled by your messy little feelings. So easy to twist them to my own ends."

He leaned in close, his breath fetid. "I'll peel back all those layers of humanity you cling to. The love, the anguish, the fear. I'll strip it all away until there's nothing left but the howling void."

I set my jaw, resolute. "You're wrong. Our emotions make us who we are. Even as vampires, they're the last echoes of the lives we left behind."

I balled my fists. "You want to break us, but you can't. Not while we stand united. Not while we have each other."

For a moment, Alice's eyes cleared, and I saw her gaze back at me with hope. But then Oblivion seized control once more, his face twisting with rage.

"We'll see about that, witch," he growled. He reached for Antoine again, murder in his eyes.

This was it. I had to break through to Alice now, or we would all be lost...

I steeled myself and shouted, "Alice, I know you're still in there! Don't let him use you like this. You're stronger than his hate, his cruelty. Fight him!"

Oblivion howled, enraged at my words. He whirled to face me, ichor dripping from his hands.

"You pathetic fool. I've already won. Soon your so-called Underground will be nothing but dust, erased from existence by my hand."

I met his glare unflinchingly. "No. You'll never win, not truly. Because no matter how much chaos and suffering you cause, it will never fill that void inside you."

I took a step towards him, emboldened. "We have something you can never understand, Oblivion—love. For each other, for our world. Yes, even for whatever remains of our *humanity*. And we will never stop fighting for it."

Suddenly, Alice's body spasmed. Her eyes flickered. She clutched her head, crying out in pain and effort.

I rushed to her side. "Alice! I know you can overpower him. Fight!"

With a guttural scream, she fell to her knees. When she looked up at me again, her eyes were clear.

"Mercy," she gasped, "he's fighting me, but I'm still here."

Relief flooded through me. I clasped her shoulder. "You did it, Alice. I knew you were stronger than him."

She managed a pained smile. "For now. But we have to be quick—I can't hold Oblivion back forever."

I nodded, resolute. "Then let's end this. Together. We just need a few days and we can bring Ladinas back."

Alice gripped my hand, her face etched with strain. "We're trapped here. Three days on earth, maybe. But time moves differently in this world. Here, we'd have to wait a hundred years before Ladinas could return."

My heart sank. I'd been so focused on surviving each moment that I had forgotten about how time was passing differently in this world. That Ladinas had only *just started* his extra century to charge up his power had slipped my mind.

"You're right," I said heavily. "We can't wait that long for Ladinas. Not here. But what if I told you that you could be with Ladinas soon? But you'd have to join him *in the lamp...*"

"With Oblivion inside of me?" Alice asked. "I don't know..."

"Ladinas is like a god in the lamp. Oblivion would be little more than a nuisance. A fly that Ladinas could swat away with little more than a thought."

"But the cupids are still on earth..."

I took Alice's hands. "I know. That's why we can't do this yet. We need you to be strong. Draw hope from the chance you'll have to be with Ladinas soon. But there's one more thing you need to know."

Alice bit her lip, uncertainty in her eyes. "What is it?"

"If we put you in the lamp with Ladinas, we can't ever let you out. Ladinas might be able to squash Oblivion while he's in the lamp world, but in a century earth-time, when the djinn returns..."

"Oblivion will leave. He'll be hellbent on vengeance."

I nodded. "Which is why we can't allow the djinn to return. When the time comes, I'll fight like hell. I'll find a way to stop him. But that means..."

"We'll be stuck in the lamp... forever..."

I nodded. "I know it's a lot to ask."

She closed her eyes. When she opened them again, they shone with purpose. "We'd be together. Not stuck. Finally free. For Ladinas, I'd give anything. Even eternity in that lamp, if it means we're together. But I can't make that choice for him."

I shook my head. "We already told Ladinas that this might be a possibility. In fact, it was his idea. He's willing to do this. He already said he'd give up the world to be with you, Alice."

Alice's resolve wavered, uncertainty clouding her eyes once more. "I want to say yes. But the cupids…"

I took her hands again, giving them a reassuring squeeze. "I know. But perhaps you can use the hope of being with Ladinas for strength. I need you to dig deep. I know you're barely holding on. But you need to take over Oblivion's power. You need to play him like the puppet he tried to make of you."

Alice took a deep breath. "To send the cupids back to where they belong. To end this nightmare. To free our friends."

"Think of Ladinas," I said. "His love for you. You can do it."

Alice grinned and put her hand on my shoulder. She grabbed the cross dangling from her neck with her other hand. "Being with Ladinas isn't the only source of my strength. I have faith. I can do this."

I smiled at Alice. I didn't share her faith, but I certainly admired it. Even if her faith had once been used against her as a pretense to turn her into a self-loathing vampire who killed other vampires. That was in the past, of course. We all made mistakes. I certainly did. And if her faith gave her what she needed to get this done, who was I to question it?

"We can't climb out of here, you know. We'll need you to take Oblivion's power before we can get free and reach the portal home."

Alice nodded. "But before I do that, I need to free our friends."

Alice turned, still clutching her cross. The power around her swirled in an impressive light show. She'd wielded celestial power once. She had appeared like an angel. But now it was as if she'd reclaimed that power—as if she'd taken Oblivion's power and refined it through the purity of her hope and faith.

With a blast of power, the ichor binding our friends burned away. One by one, they came to. Antoine, Clement, Ian and the other orphans. All of them—except those who Oblivion had already... erased...

Alice's eyes brimmed with tears as she took a step closer to the first vampire to regain consciousness. She wiped away Antoine's tears with a trembling hand, her voice wavering as she whispered, "We're not home yet, Antoine. But you're safe. The nightmare is over."

With every vampire that blinked open their eyes and found themselves no longer trapped in that sticky, foul-smelling ichor, Alice's resolve strengthened. This was more than just a fight for the Underground. It was a fight for hope, for love, and for the very essence of what it meant to be alive.

I was at a loss for words. When Alice turned around, blazing in power, I practically choked on my tongue. "You did it! I can't believe it!"

"I told you," Alice smiled at me. "My faith works."

"I don't know about your religion…"

"It doesn't matter," Alice said. "Whether you believe in God or not, today, *you* were my angel. And I see it clearly now. Despite all we've been through. You've *always* been my angel."

I didn't have words to respond. I wasn't a hugger—but the emotion of the moment overwhelmed me. Not the kind of emotion Oblivion could use against me, either. I wrapped my arms around Alice. "Let's get home and end this once and for all."

Chapter 19

THE LIGHT WAS BLINDING as Alice emerged from the portal, her wings spread wide. No longer leathery like a dragon's, they now glowed pearly white, feathers rustling. She was magnificent.

I shielded my eyes as Alice gathered us up, her magic pulling me and the others from that wretched dimension. The familiar scents of the Ridley washed over me.

Alice wasted no time. She let us fall to the carpeted floor, then brushed past without a word, her body shifting as she moved. Delicate scales rippled across her skin, shimmering white and iridescent. She flung open the front doors and stepped outside.

Alice didn't require kevlar. I still had my suit. I dropped my visor over my eyes to protect myself from the light.

Alice announced her return to the world with a primal roar. I hurried after her, stunned by the sight that greeted me. Cupids—thousands of them—streamed through the sky toward Alice, their wings beating furiously. She stood with arms upraised, catching their small bodies as they dove into her breath.

I knew what she was doing. Sending them home, using Oblivion's power to do it. She had found hope, faith, and love. And it had given her the strength to suppress the dragon within.

But for how long? Oblivion lurked under the surface, biding his time. We still needed to retrieve the lamp. To find a way to contain him more permanently.

A flash of rainbow light nearly blinded me. I blinked, and Pauli was perched on my shoulder, tongue flicking, scales glinting.

"Miss me?" he said, then dissolved into laughter at my startled expression.

Before I could respond, the air swirled with emerald motes. They coalesced into Muggs, with Juliet, Hailey, Mel, and Goliath at his side.

Juliet rushed forward and kissed my cheek. "What happened?" she asked, pink hair tousled, concern in her dark eyes.

I sighed. "It's a long story."

I gave her an abbreviated summary—Alice defeating Oblivion by embracing love, by relying on her faith, but the demon still lurking within.

Muggs nodded solemnly. "We must retrieve the lamp. I've hidden it away, protected by powerful enchantments."

I rolled my eyes. "I know exactly where it is. The same damned place I found Oblivion and Alice."

His eyes widened in surprise. "I should have known. To think we could traverse worlds and a dragon wouldn't know it."

"An oversight on our part," I admitted. "And it cost us a few of our own. Oblivion killed some of our best soldiers before Alice took control."

Muggs shook his head as he watched Alice. "This isn't wise, Mercy. If Oblivion already killed some of our team, what kind of rage will he unleash if he gets free again? How long do you think Alice can keep that dragon leashed?"

"I don't know," I admitted. "But she's agreed to the plan. She doesn't want to spend the rest of her life fighting against Oblivion, either. We need to take her to Ladinas."

Juliet slipped her hand in mine, gaze troubled as she watched Alice on the street below.

"She's killing them, isn't she?" Juliet asked quietly. "The cupids."

I squeezed her hand. "She's sending them home. Wherever that might be."

It was a small comfort, but hope was in short supply of late. We had to take it where we could find it.

"Alice knows what must be done?" Muggs asked. "She understands that she and Ladinas will have to keep Oblivion in that lamp with them forever?"

I met his gaze steadily. "She's ready."

Muggs stroked his beard thoughtfully. "That djinn is going to give us one hell of a fight in a century when he realizes what we've done."

I laughed. "Well, in a century, we'll all be stronger and wiser. Plus, we have a hundred years to hammer out our plan. It'll be nice to be prepared for the bad guy for once."

Juliet tightened her grip on my hand. I surveyed the streets ahead, watched as Alice dispatched the last of the cupids in a flash of light.

Juliet interlaced her fingers with mine as we watched Alice finish sending the cupids back to their realm. I felt the brush of her pink hair against my cheek as she leaned her head on my shoulder, seeking a moment of quiet connection amidst the chaos.

"I love you," she whispered, her voice thick with emotion.

My cold heart swelled. Vampires didn't blush, but if we could, my face would be flaming right about now. I turned and pressed a gentle kiss to her hair.

"I love you too, Juliet."

The words were inadequate for the depth of feeling between us, which was a lot more than a *feeling* now.

Muggs cleared his throat, breaking the spell of the tender moment. "I may have a solution. A pocket dimension where we can seal the lamp. Time moves much slower there. Ten thousand years will pass for every one of ours."

I barked out a laugh. "That's about as close to forever as we're gonna get. I think that'll do nicely."

The cornstalks rustled as we made our way through the lamp world. Muggs led the way, with Juliet's hand clasped firmly in mine. Alice brought up the rear, her steps slow and hesitant.

A young girl suddenly burst from the crops ahead, barreling towards us at full speed.

"Mommy!" she cried, flinging herself into Alice's arms.

Alice laughed, surprise and delight chasing away the shadows in her eyes. "Well, I don't know about that, but I'd sure like to be!"

The girl giggled and squeezed Alice tight. My dead heart lurched a little in my chest.

I tore my gaze away, only to meet familiar crimson eyes watching me from up ahead. Ladinas. Still wearing that damn Michael Landon getup, suspenders and all.

Alice saw him at the same moment I did. With a joyful shout, she sprinted forward, leaping into his waiting arms. They clung to each other, lost in their reunion.

When they finally parted, Alice's expression had fallen somber.

"Oblivion is inside me," she said urgently. "We have to get him out."

Ladinas nodded, unsurprised. Of course, he already knew. Extending one hand, a glass jar materialized from nowhere. He passed it to the little girl.

"Open this, Beatrice. You're getting a new pet."

The girl's eyes went wide. She fumbled eagerly with the lid.

Ladinas touched Alice's chest. A soft glow emanated from within. Alice gasped, then slumped against him in relief.

When Ladinas withdrew his hand, he held a tiny, writhing dragon. With a flick of his wrist, he dropped it into the waiting jar.

Beatrice quickly screwed the lid back on. "Don't you worry, little guy! I'll take good care of you!"

Ladinas smiled indulgently. Just like that, Oblivion was contained. Alice was free.

Alice turned to me, eyes bright with emotion. "Thank you, Mercy. For everything. I can't tell you what this means to me."

I nodded, swallowing the sudden lump in my throat. "I'm happy for you, Alice. You deserve this."

And she did. After centuries of violence and heartache, my recent friend and long-time nemesis had finally found peace. Part of me envied the simple life she and Ladinas would have here.

No more battles to fight, no more blood to spill. Just... existence.

Enjoying each moment as it came.

But that kind of life wasn't meant for me. Not yet, anyway. There were still vampires, an entire world full of people who needed protecting. There were more wars to wage, more dangers to thwart. I wasn't done fighting.

Maybe someday, after it was all over, Juliet and I could carve out a slice of forever for ourselves too. But that might not come for centuries.

So be it. I loved my existence the way it was. I didn't need a lamp world to find peace.

Real serenity isn't what you feel when everything's peachy keen. It's what you experience when the whole world is going to shit, but you're content.

I met Ladinas's knowing gaze. "Take care of her," I said gruffly.

He inclined his head. "Always. This might be the beginning of our forever, but it doesn't mean it has to be our forever goodbye. You're always welcome here."

"We might just take you up on that," I said gruffly. "But any chance you could make your world something a little less Nebraska and a little more Cabo San Lucas the next time we come visit?"

Ladinas laughed. "That can be arranged. When can I expect you next?"

I shrugged. "You never know. The next time we get a little break from world-ending threats, maybe? That could be tomorrow. It might take a few years. But I can't leave you two lovebirds alone for too long. Who knows what trouble you'll get up to."

Alice laughed, bright and carefree. The sound warmed me. After everything she had suffered, she deserved a little laughter.

With a last goodbye, I turned and put my arm around Juliet. Muggs spun his staff and took us home. Back to the Underground.

My battles weren't over. But for Alice, the war was won.

The End of Book 7
To Be Continued in *Bloody Moon*
Want more Hailey and Pauli? Check out The Blood Witch Saga

Also By Theophilus Monroe

Gates of Eden Universe

In recommended reading order...

The Druid Legacy
Druid's Dance
Bard's Tale
Ovate's Call
Rise of the Morrigan

The Fomorian Wyrmriders
Wyrmrider Ascending
Wyrmrider Vengeance
Wyrmrider Justice
Wyrmrider Academy (Exclusive to Omnibus Edition)

The Voodoo Legacy

Voodoo Academy
Grim Tidings
Death Rites
Watery Graves
Voodoo Queen

The Legacy of a Vampire Witch
Bloody Hell
Bloody Mad
Bloody Wicked
Bloody Devils
Bloody Gods

The Legend of Nyx
Scared Shiftless
Bat Shift Crazy
No Shift, Sherlock
Shift for Brains
Shift Happens
Shift on a Shingle

The Vilokan Asylum of the Magically and Mentally Deranged
The Curse of Cain
The Mark of Cain
Cain and the Cauldron
Cain's Cobras

Crazy Cain
The Wrath of Cain

The Blood Witch Saga
Voodoo and Vampires
Witches and Wolves
Devils and Dragons
Ghouls and Grimoires
Faeries and Fangs
Monsters and Mambos
Wraiths and Warlocks
Shifters and Shenanigans

The Fury of a Vampire Witch
Bloody Queen
Bloody Underground
Bloody Retribution
Bloody Bastards
Bloody Brilliance
Bloody Merry
Bloody Hearts
Bloody Moon
Bloody Fortune
Bloody Rebels
More to come!

The Druid Detective Agency

Merlin's Mantle
Roundtable Nights
Grail of Power
Midsummer Monsters
Stones and Bones
The Wild Hunt
More to come!

Sebastian Winter
Death to All Monsters
More to come!

Other Theophilus Monroe Series

Nanoverse

The Elven Prophecy

Chronicles of Zoey Grimm

The Daywalker Chronicles

Go Ask Your Mother

The Hedge Witch Diaries

AS T.R. MAGNUS

Kataklysm
Blightmage
Ember
Radiant
Dreadlord
Deluge

About the Author

Theophilus Monroe is a fantasy author with a knack for real-life characters whose supernatural experiences speak to the pangs of ordinary life. After earning his Ph.D. in Theology, he decided that academic treatises that no one will read (beyond other academics) was a dull way to spend his life. So, he began using his background in religious studies to create new worlds and forms of magic–informed by religious myths, ancient and modern–that would intrigue readers, inspire imaginations, and speak to real-world problems in fantastical ways.

When Theophilus isn't exploring one of his fantasy lands, he is probably playing with one of his three sons, or pumping iron in his home gym, which is currently located in a 40-foot shipping container.

He makes his online home at www.theophilusmonroe.com. He loves answering reader questions—feel free to e-mail him at theophilus@theophilusmonroe.com if the mood strikes you!

Printed in Great Britain
by Amazon